THE GARDEN OF UNFORTUNATE SOULS

EDDIE MARK

booktrope

Booktrope Editions
Seattle, WA 2015

Cover Design by Scott Deyett
Edited by Gerald Braude

This is a work of fiction. Names, characters, places, brands, media, and incidents are either the product of the author's imagination or are used fictitiously. Any resemblance to similarly named places or to persons living or deceased is unintentional.

PRINT ISBN 978-1-62015-793-0
EPUB ISBN 978-1-62015-812-8
Library of Congress Control Number: 2015905264

ACKNOWLEDGMENTS

A published book is not the creation of any one individual. As such, I wish to thank the many talented people who supported this effort along the way: the entire team at Booktrope, especially Sárka-Jonae Miller, Mary Ward Menke, Scott Deyett, Beth Bacon, Annie St. John, Jesse James Freeman, Adam Bodendieck, and of course my editor Gerald Braude, without whose expertise and insight this novel wouldn't be worth reading; Magdalen Powers for her tips on gardens and grammar (I took many liberties, none of which should be blamed on her); Alan R. Core and Charles Castiglia for answering my questions about the funeral business (again, I took many liberties, none of which should be blamed on them); my friend Virginie Salles over in Europe for fact-checking my Spanish; Edwidge Danticat, who, many years ago, graciously found nice things to say about a horribly written chapter called *How I Got You Off My Mind*; Dr. Willis Beardsley for giving me confidence; my good friend Matthew Newuiett, Buffalo's greatest librarian, for introducing me to the works of the great fiction masters; and Dr. Charles Johnson, brilliant writer and academic, not only for his endorsement, but also for his selfless generosity and encouragement, and for believing in me when many others did not. I am forever indebted. And finally, much love to my mom and dad, two fascinating people who are both so clever with words. All I have ever wanted was to make them proud.

For Thabitha,
because you said it would be, and it is

If abuse, like a weed, be cut down by the scythe of neglect, it will die of itself.

—THOMAS BRYDSON

1

It happened on a rainy Friday night in April, in the spring of 1987. Loretta had already prayed and dressed for bed when a young man named Audwin Brooks, the mayor's son, drove straight into the railing of her front porch. This was not a deliberate act he would later claim in a compulsory handwritten letter addressed to The Lady at 99 Peach Street, Buffalo, New York, but an accident he could not control. Caught in a storm that night, hurtling through thundershowers, fog, and gusts of a forty-mile-an-hour wind, his tires had lost traction as he made the sharp turn onto her street, and before he could catch the wheel—before he could even react—he had jumped the curb and swerved across the yard into the railing.

"Downright shameful," Loretta said to herself. "Not even a real apology." And so the letter went the way of all junk mail, as nothing it explained could ease the stress of having seen a car halted at her porch stairs with cracked headlights and a dented fender pressed against the wrought iron railing. The front post had survived the impact, but was crooked now and no longer sturdy, and the balusters—each of them an elegant vermiform scroll like serpents spiraling to a kiss—were so unsteady no one could feel secure about climbing those stairs. Much worse, Loretta couldn't even look upon her garden. For a lane now struck through the boxwood hedge she had labored hard to maintain, an unsightly gap where the young man's car had plowed through and carved a trail of tire marks into her new grass—and had shattered the gnome and crushed the tulips, and flattened to the mulch the lemon-yellow daffodils she loved to touch. A tragedy, because 99 was the only house on the block that even had a real garden. And now Loretta, a woman of limited means, having no extra money for repairs, could only wonder what she was going to do—what she could *possibly* do—about the damage to her garden and front porch.

But perhaps the most troubling thing about that Friday night (more than being broke and unable to accept the charity of the mayor himself when he offered) was that Shadrack, her otherwise shrewd twelve-year-old boy, had somehow slept through the noise. He hadn't stirred at all. So the next morning she took him to have his hearing checked, and though the doctor said nothing was wrong and that Shadrack's ears were fine, Loretta was not convinced. And for years after the crash, each time she scolded him and he failed to respond, or she warned him about some silly girl and he didn't listen, she figured he had gone deaf in one ear at some point and couldn't hear much of anything.

Though forever strange to Loretta that Shadrack hadn't heard what she heard that night, she already knew he lived in a world where such events registered little effect—a world whose door was sealed and padlocked (at least that's what Loretta had told him), so there was no use in trying to push it open. Aside from church, school, and brief monitored trips to the bathroom toilet (when Loretta finally felt the urge to let him go) and the kitchen table (when Loretta finally hungered for some dinner), Shadrack languished in his upstairs bedroom, staring back at a gloomy window shade that shut out everything, which was only fitting because he wasn't allowed to look outside anyway. Though he might have longed to watch the neighborhood kids run free, their adventures undoubtedly reeling out like a silent movie before him, he was never one to be disobedient, and simply missed it all.

Loretta couldn't name the hour this infirmity had first come upon her son, nor did she know the precise extent of it. But when the thunderstorm came, and the crash happened, and not even a whisper of that commotion echoed in Shadrack's ears, she was most determined to get him some help and whatever hearing aids he required.

At first light of day, the day after the crash, before there was any sound or movement in the streets of their neighborhood, Loretta marched him through early morning fog and wet roads to the Emergency Room at Buffalo General, where she explained everything. How there had always been times when Shadrack had problems paying attention. Moments he was oblivious to any swirl of excitement, and seemed to possess, even at age twelve, the sad countenance of an enfeebled old man. But she had never known his spirit to be so lifeless that not even a car crash against the house could rouse him from sleep.

"There's something wrong with this boy," Loretta said to Dr. Feldman. "If the Rapture happened right now, he wouldn't even look up to see it. Now, I might not be a doctor, but I'm a mother, and I know something ain't right."

Dr. Feldman, a large man perched on a small stool, uttered a sigh, telling Loretta that the only thing he could do now was repeat himself. Because he found nothing wrong with Shadrack's ears. They were fine. Both of them. But he *did* happen to notice the burns on his scalp and the welts that rippled along the backs of his legs.

"He earned those," Loretta said. "With his misbehaviors."

Dr. Feldman furrowed his brow. "You whip him so much?"

"I do what the Bible says to do," she said, proud that the signs of her corrective parenting were so noticeable.

"You know, Miss Ford, we understand single parents deal with a lot of stress sometimes—"

"You understand, or you read that somewhere?"

"What I'm saying is that nowadays people are starting to frown on this kind of discipline."

"Frown all you want," Loretta said. "It don't faze me none. Do as you please in your own home. As for *my* home we follow scripture."

"Where does it say to welt a child's body like this?"

"Beg your pardon?"

"These bruises are all over his body, Miss Ford. I asked what Bible verse says to do that."

But Loretta grabbed Shadrack's wrist and left, leaving her adversary to figure it out for himself because a man who didn't know the Bible wasn't worth the time it took to explain.

The Erie County Child Protective Services agent who arrived at the house later was less cynical than Dr. Feldman and saw no reason why a boy being reared in a decent Christian home would ever come to harm. She checked and found ample food in the pantry. Sufficient red meat in the freezer. Observed Shadrack's good English and good manners and decided all was reasonable at 99 Peach Street, especially since this struggling young mother was raising him without any help.

Loretta Ford, unmarried, earning a scanty wage as a cashier at Super Duper, was now twenty-eight. She had come to Buffalo back in the seventies as a mere teenager from a small tract of country land called Manning, South Carolina—pregnant and traveling alone, leaving behind a full grave's worth of bad memories, after having decided that a woman only comes of age once she's had her world cracked and shattered by some man. She and Shadrack now lived in a part of town called the Fruit Belt, so named for the lovely orchards German settlers had cultivated there over a century before. Those humble refugees—Lutherans—had come pursuing freedom to practice their faith, and established a church and built a community all around it adorned with fruit trees and lavish flower gardens. Decades passed, a century passed, and now it was a neighborhood of old-fashioned gable-front houses and arbored streets that still bore the names of fruit trees, though the orchards and Germans were no longer there—streets called Grape, Lemon, Orange, Beech, Cherry, Maple, Locust, Mulberry, and Peach.

These avenues lay on the periphery of the downtown core, east of the Allentown nightlife scene and mere walking distance from the Anchor Bar where Buffalo wings were rumored to have been invented in 1964 when the proprietor discovered she had nothing else to serve one night and improvised her way into history with trays of deep-fried chicken wings flavored with a spiced up hot sauce—a dish now offered on nearly every restaurant menu in the world. A few blocks the other way, at Broadway and Michigan, stood the Colored Musicians Club with its classic upright pianos and 1920s Harlem Renaissance décor. Its walls were lined with photos of legends such as Billie Holiday, Count Basie, and Duke Ellington—all of whom had flaunted their chops up in the second floor loft whenever they came to town.

But that was many years ago, when Buffalo was still a great hub of excitement in the northeast. Long before the manufacturing industry contracted and stifled all economic optimism in the region. With jobs and money scarce, Buffalonians by the tens of thousands had begun to set their gazes southward and westward, jamming up the outbound interstates trying to escape the plague of poverty overtaking the city. And neighborhoods such as the Fruit Belt that had once been proudly middle class, hopelessly watched their property values sink to the bottom of Lake Erie. Thus the Fruit Belt became the stomping ground of the unemployed and the working-poor, many of whom staffed whichever local establishments had not yet closed: The Blessed Home Funeral Parlor, Hassan's Liquor Store, the Hunt Senior Center on Locust, the Lemon Street Convenience Mart, a nursing home, three churches, Fat Larry's

Soul Food Barbecue, the Nu-Do Hair Salon, an armory, a bakery, a home daycare on Cherry Street, and Al Taylor's Check-n-Cash where on the first and fifteenth of every month the line stretched out the door and down the block.

And then there were those who were neither unemployed nor working-poor—the never employed, as it were—who boycotted the concept of conventional work altogether. For they had long ago made the calculation that free time, though immensely unprofitable, still carried more intrinsic value than any number of hours times three dollars and thirty-five cents. Theirs was the sin of contentment, not poverty. For having little money was forgivable in Loretta's book (after all, she was broke, and Jesus himself was poor). But these newer residents were perfectly fine having nothing, perfectly proud of having landed in some perverse paradise of low expectations. Moreover, they possessed no thirst for those elusive better days when, say, new Cadillacs motored through the Fruit Belt instead of noisy jalopies leaking oil and souring the neighborhood air with the rotten-egg scent of bad carburetors—better days, a mere few years ago, when the local elementary school didn't have bars on its windows, and a man wouldn't stab his buddy in the throat over a two dollar dispute: the days before crack cocaine and rap music and girls wearing pants two sizes too small for their hips; before teenage boys sporting gold chains, thinking nothing of shooting some pedestrian from the open window of a stolen SUV. Nay, these folks were not sinners because they were less fortunate. They were sinners because they always *would* be, and Loretta had no tolerance for that mindset.

At times when she found herself out front, kneeling before the flowerbed, thinning out the shoots of her perennials, she watched her neighbors from the corner of her eye but never spoke, and merely looked away whenever they sought her attention.

"Ungodly fools, every one of them," she would mumble to herself. "Headed straight for hell and pretend they don't know it." She had grown tired of their foul mouths and idle porch sitting; their untended, weed-ridden lawns; the broken gutters and screen doors that hung off the hinges. The fights, the noise, the burglaries. These were a different breed altogether. Before them, gardens and homes were well-kept. Quiet, courteous people lived in them. Homeowners, not squatters and gigolos. Church folk. Preachers and such. But the Fruit Belt had become a place where preachers no longer cared to dwell. Because ever since an elderly minister, a revered community man who once hosted Martin Luther King at his home, was found robbed and murdered in the vestibule of the Mulberry Street Sanctuary of Praise—shot dead by members of a street gang dubbed the Fruit Belt Posse—most of the ministers had moved their families out of the neighborhood for good. Many of the other residents had done the same, reasoning no one was safe anywhere if preachers weren't safe in church. So by the time Audwin Brooks came careening onto Loretta Ford's front lawn in the spring of 1987, many of the houses on that end of Peach Street were already empty and boarded up, and her only remaining neighbors were the very people she did her best to avoid.

She still doubted any of them realized, or even cared, what happened that Friday night in April when a thunderstorm had left the streets of her neighborhood deserted past midnight. The noise of the collision had caused some neighbor's dog to bark in the rain, and a few windows on the block lit up, but no one came outside—which was not unusual in the Fruit Belt on a night like this—and it was perfectly fine with Loretta. She had already warned them to mind their own business when it came to the affairs of 99 Peach Street. So even on a night when someone had driven a car into her front porch, her neighbors (even if they had caught a vague glimpse of something) would have known to stay out of it and quietly turn their lights back out.

Loretta was awake when it happened. When she heard the crash, she hurried down to the living room, leaving Shadrack asleep upstairs. She drew apart the front curtain and stared out. A young man was in the car struggling with the ignition, but the engine wouldn't crank, though it didn't matter anyway because a front tire had blown out and wouldn't travel even if the snarling engine somehow sprang alive. The night was blustery and wet. Billows of rain swept down across the swaying treetops and over the streets. And the neighborhood, dark and beclouded, was only sparsely illuminated by the hazy yellow crowns of streetlamp light that shone through the murk.

When the young man gave up and the snarling noise of his car ceased, Loretta watched him shove open the car door and stagger out into the rain—a disoriented, lanky young man, dressed in a leather jacket with the collar turned up, his uncovered head now drenched and pitiful like some whimpering stray animal. She thought to call the police right away. But when he fell to his knees and coughed blood into the grass, Loretta threw on her raincoat and did what anyone from her church would have done and hurried out to help him.

She scampered into the night, shielding her face from the rush of a driving wet wind, and she could see he was unsteady, slipping each time his bony knees raised up from a miry mud puddle in the grass. "Are you hurt?" Loretta said, crouching beside him. Gurgling cold water soaked her slippers. "Are you hurt?" she said again, louder.

Still coughing and trying to raise up from his knees, the young man uttered something inaudible through the clamor of thundershowers and wind. Loretta saw streaks of red on his cheek. Splotches of coughed blood out of the left side of his mouth. "Come on," she said. "You can't stay out here like this." Loretta curled his leather arm over her shoulders and helped him stand, and then guided him into the house where he suddenly heaved and vomited onto her living room carpet.

"Good Lord," Loretta said, lurching back.

She smelled whiskey.

The young man heaved again, and after wiping his mouth with his sleeve, he trudged over to the sofa and plopped down, sprawling with his head flung back as if he had given up his soul. Loretta retrieved two rags from the kitchen, some ice cubes, saltwater, and an empty pitcher she mostly used for Shadrack's Kool-Aid. She cleaned the young man's cheeks and nudged his head forward to rinse and spit into the pitcher. When she checked his mouth, he had all of his teeth. The blood had only come from a deeply reddened tongue laceration that was still welling up.

"Here, stick out your tongue," Loretta said. She placed a damp rag on the cut. Her face hovered ever so close to his, and she could sense his gaze following her every move. When the bleeding slowed, she wrapped the other rag around some ice cubes and raised it to his mouth. This time the young man snatched the rag and applied it himself.

Rather handsome, Loretta thought, observing his clean schoolboy features and a pair of chestnut brown eyes that were quite striking, though bloodshot and woozy at the moment. He wore a high-top fade, flawlessly shaped and tapered, as from meticulous grooming, but had the thin, airy physique of a young man not quite grown, the clueless, slump-shouldered posture of a teenager not more than sixteen or seventeen.

When a powerful drowsiness fell over him, the young man dozed off, spilling the bloodstained rag and ice cubes from his hand. Loretta removed his jacket and sneakers, and propped his head on a throw pillow, then went to her knees to scrub away the vomit and muddy footprints in her carpet. When she finished, she checked on Shadrack, who was still asleep upstairs, still in the same supine position as when he first lay down earlier, wholly unaltered in his bed as if it were his casket.

Loretta leaned against the doorjamb, watching him. A slab of hallway light cast her shadow over his undersized, twelve-year-old body. "Shadrack," she whispered into the dark. "You up, son?" But he didn't respond, and his rhythmic breathing never broke stride.

Though concerned, Loretta was not surprised. Other late-night incidents had already exposed his disability. Indeed, through all her violent tussles with her ex-boyfriends, her son had slept. Did the same during a police raid on a drug house nearby. When sirens wailed, Shadrack snored. When car alarms blared, he was at peace. Never once flinched at the crackle of gunfire outside the house or the pandemonium of a three-alarm blaze on Grape Street, the next block over.

When Loretta drew close and poked his shoulder, Shadrack shifted a little but never woke. "Strange," Loretta whispered. "Mighty strange."

Around 2:00 a.m., the young man in the living room stirred. Loretta was seated at the other end of the couch, still in her raincoat, staring as he gradually became lucid. When he saw her, he sat up and stared back.

"You always let strangers in your house?" he said, and immediately he expressed pain, as of a throbbing soreness in his head.

"I never let anyone in my house," Loretta said. She slid a mug of ice water across the coffee table. "Get some water in your system. Flush out all that liquor."

The young man dropped his forehead into the palms of his hands. "You have any aspirin?"

"That won't help none. You'd probably just throw up again. Drink some water."

Painfully, slowly, the young man peered up at Loretta and studied her. "Who are you, lady?"

"Well," Loretta said casually, "I'm the owner of the house that got in your way a little while ago. Real question is who are *you*?"

"I'm sure you went through my pockets already."

Loretta smirked. "My life ain't that empty."

"Then why do you need to know who I am?

"Standard question, I reckon. You crashed into my house, threw up on my carpet, then fell asleep on my couch. Figure it's about time I at least know your name."

The young man dropped his head again. Outside, the rain and wind had fallen quiet, though a lingering breeze still rattled the windowpane. A rap song played from a car that had momentarily idled a few houses down, no doubt attending to some covert late-night business. Its tires screeched away shortly after.

"You chewed your tongue real bad," Loretta said. "Feel any other pains? Thought maybe I should call an ambulance to be safe. In case you got injured and don't know."

"Everything's fine," he said. "I'm leaving. Pass me the phone. I'll call my father."

"Your daddy a doctor or something?"

The young man held out his hand. "Lady, please. Just pass me the phone."

A grumbling, beaten-down old tow truck lumbered its way onto Peach Street and Loretta's front lawn. When its flaring lights beamed through the living room curtains, the young man hustled out of the house without a word. Loretta followed out to the porch, watching as a rough-bearded trucker attached the yoke to the car and hoisted it up. He towed it away with the young man riding with him. It happened that quickly. Loretta had wanted to say something before he left. Exactly what she wanted to articulate, she didn't know, but something.

The barking dog was silent now, and the night was presided over by an immense purplish-black sky that had within it no glimmer of starlight or moon. The car had left behind an odor of antifreeze. Or maybe it was engine oil or transmission fluid. Maybe even fuel. She couldn't tell the difference. But she reasoned that a lot of it must have leaked onto her new grass, which now had muddy tire marks in it. Moreover, her pretty tulips and daffodils were trampled over and ruined. Loretta, standing alone by the crooked railing in dim porch light beneath a murky black sky, her mood miserably soured by all of this, simply crimped her lips and shook her head.

She was about to head back in when a set of high beam headlights veered onto her street. A luxury car of a foreign make crept up to the curb in front of her house. It paused there beneath a streetlamp as a dusky silhouette looked to confirm the address. A man in a black trench coat stepped from the car and waved as if Loretta had been expecting him. He was tall and calm-gaited (no doubt the father or lawyer of the young man who had just left), and his expensive shoes clapped against the wet pavement as he ambled up the driveway to her porch. Loretta didn't like the scent of air he brought with him. The rude confidence of his stride. The presumptuousness. The inevitable pompous demand for an explanation of what had transpired there that night. But what she hadn't expected, once he stepped into a slant of porch light and she could see him better, was that she would instantly recognize his face, which she did. For the man who stood before her at the crooked railing, grinning as though not actually imposing, was Cornelius Brooks, the twice-elected mayor of Buffalo—a man whose dignity seemed out of place in her presence and made her feel somewhat out of place in his. The mere sight of him made her shoulders stiffen, such that when he removed his gloves and held out his palm, Loretta only reluctantly shook it, surprised at once by the peculiar softness of such powerful hands.

"Bit of a mess here," the mayor said. He briefly surveyed the front lawn. "Do you know who I am?"

Loretta nodded. "People wondered what it would take to get you down here." Whiffs of their warm breath rose into the night air. "It's late," she said. "What can I do for you?"

The mayor mounted the stairs so that now Loretta had clear sight of his photogenic face. He was more handsome in person than on television, but the being within him seemed fatigued somehow, as if he had hauled a great burden up to her doorstep. "We need to talk for a minute," he said, gesturing toward her open door. "Privately, if you don't mind."

Though the night breeze blew cold and it made sense to go inside, Loretta didn't move, and stood with her arms folded against her bosom as if guarding the entrance to the house. She harbored no dislike for the mayor. He was a respected man, after all. She just wasn't in the mood for any more company that night, and besides, you don't let the mayor of Buffalo walk into your home without cleaning up first.

"Think people won't notice me out here?" he said. And without waiting for a reply, he asked, "You know that was my son Audwin, right?"

"I know now," Loretta said. "He didn't say his name."

"Was he rude?"

"Being a kid I guess."

"He happen to mention what he was doing down here?"

Loretta shrugged. "He didn't say much. But this time a night, I'd reckon it was on account of a girl. High-class boys always sneak down here after dark."

"We're not high-class."

A breeze sprinkled down leftover rainwater from the treetops. Peach Street was empty. Noiseless. Even the worst hated rain, Loretta had decided long ago. Let it snow one night, and you'd wake to find bloodstains on the ice. Send the rain, and the street corners stayed quiet until morning.

"Have any kids?" the mayor said.

"Just one. Shadrack."

"And *your* name?"

When Loretta told him, he nodded and told her to address him by his first name as well. He then began a series of apologies for his son, and also for the inconvenience, and assured her he and his wife, Bernadine, would make up for it.

"Accidents happen," Loretta said. "Long as he's all right, that's fine with me. But I tell you, I wanted to call an ambulance just in case—"

"No need," the mayor said abruptly. "He's okay. We appreciate your help." He pointed to the stair railing. "We'll have somebody come fix everything for you. Won't even know the difference. "

"Thanks kindly," Loretta said. With the matter now settled, she hoped he would leave, but he gave no such indication. A Cutlass swerved onto Peach Street (around the same sharp corner the mayor's son must have come earlier) and made its way down the block, splashing water from a pothole and veering onto Carlton Street toward Orange. Loretta doubted the driver even noticed them standing out there. "Oh, and I smelled whiskey on him," she said.

The mayor chuckled. "My boy doesn't drink."

"I smelled it sure enough."

"Well, I guess that's where we disagree, Loretta. I know one hundred percent Audwin doesn't drink, and certainly didn't drink tonight."

"I'm not trying to judge anybody—"

"Then there's no need for accusations," he said. "Don't say things you can't prove."

Loretta took offense to the mayor's sudden seriousness—the lofty self-righteousness, as if he himself had created man and earth in six days and rested on the seventh. She passed over his comment and glanced out at the foggy road and the foreign car, resenting the suggestion that she was somehow answerable to him. Not because she planned to tell anyone what happened that night, but because no self-respecting woman would let any man, even if he *is* the mayor, show up in the middle of the night and talk down to her. "Fine," she said. "All I did was help."

"And we're grateful for that," he said. "There's no animosity here—"

"So you want me to keep my mouth shut, that right?"

The mayor jiggled his eyebrows and smiled. "I won't sugarcoat it, Loretta. We're both parents. Sometimes you have to be discreet, if you know what I mean. The way I see it, Audwin's shaken up, but it's not serious. You've got some damage to your property. We'll take care of it. So there's no reason to make something out of nothing. You agree?"

"Like I said, you want me to keep quiet. Fine. I didn't want to be mixed up in it anyway."

"Mixed up in what exactly, Loretta? What do you mean by that?"

"This," she said. "You and your son. Everybody knows I mind my own business. He needed help, so I helped him. Figured maybe someday he'll help somebody. Far as being discreet or whatever, I already helped as much as I can. Leave me out of it."

"All right," the mayor said, sounding as if that answer was good enough for now. "Let me give you something for the trouble. Something for you and your boy." Loretta watched him pull a billfold from his trousers pocket and peel off five fresh one hundred dollar bills. He held them in front of her. "For you and Shadrack," he said. "For the trouble."

Loretta slid her hands into the pockets of her raincoat.

"Come on now, Loretta. Take it. If your neighbors see this, who knows what they'll think?"

Times were tough. Loretta hadn't bought groceries for the week yet. Shadrack needed a new Easter suit. And the electricity could go out any day now. But she had learned long ago that money comes at a high price when a woman's hand reaches for it. So she refused and politely looked past him out onto the shadows of Peach Street. "Guess you figure a poor woman like me would do anything for that money," she said. "I'm a Christian, sir. You can't pay me to lie. Nobody can."

"I never asked you to lie."

"But that's what you want."

The mayor stuffed the money back into his pocket. "Forget it."

"I can take care of me and my son," Loretta said. "Go take care of yours. And don't worry about my property either."

As far as she was concerned, as the mayor walked off, other things were of greater import now anyway, foremost was the path of her dispassionate twelve-year-old boy, who was sleeping upstairs and had apparently turned a deaf ear to the world and gone his own way. But truly, most assuredly, there would be no such rebellion in her home.

2

What Shadrack *did* hear one morning at sunrise, when he woke up soaked by the wetness of his own urine, was the noise of his mother shouting his name and commanding him to get up. When Shadrack rolled over, Loretta towered at his bedside, holding out a mop bucket and some toilet paper.

"I smelled your piss all the way across the hall," she said in a tone Shadrack knew and feared. "You animal. Next time you have to go, use this." She flung the bucket at him. It dropped to the hardwood floor and rumbled across the room, a room that had nothing in it now but four bare walls and a twin bed, because his bedwetting had provoked Loretta to take everything away. Some time ago, she had barged in and took his television. Later she returned for the Spiderman comics and the remote control car. When he defied her still—kept wetting the bed when she warned him not to—she whipped his backside with an extension cord and tore his Michael Jackson posters from the wall.

"I can't help it, Mama," Shadrack said. "It comes out when I'm asleep."

"You telling me you can't control your own body?"

"Sometimes I dream I'm at the toilet, and it comes out."

Loretta hurled the toilet paper at his face. "I don't care about no dreams." She dragged him from the bed by the crook of his arm. His knees thumped against the hardwood floor. "You *can* help it," she said. "Get up." When he stood, she slapped him, and he stumbled back to the floor. "Hard as I work to buy you things, this is how you thank me? I said get up." Loretta seized his pajama collar and hoisted him up, striking him again.

Shadrack shielded his head with his forearms and started wailing.

"Shut up! I'm done playing with you, Shadrack." Loretta whisked away the bed cover and thrust his face to the wet urine stain on the mattress.

Shadrack couldn't raise his head. The more he struggled, the firmer Loretta held his face to the stain. It was at these times he was prone to feeling weightless, going somewhere different altogether. He could hear Loretta yelling, but he had lost touch with her voice. There was no floor anymore. No walls to block the cold or the feeling of soaring on a swift wind. And he wondered what would stop him from pulling back that window shade and leaping out.

"Act like an animal, I'll treat you like one," Loretta said. She slung him back to the floor where he lay in fetal position at her feet. "Next time, I'll set your mattress outside so the whole world can see the stains. That what you want?"

Shadrack said nothing.

"You don't know how hard it is on me, Shadrack." She sounded as if she, too, wanted to cry. "Sometimes I wish I never had you . . . that you was never even born."

On Easter Sunday, while Loretta and Shadrack prepared for church, a gray rain fell the entire morning and dampened further the already soggy mood inside the house. When a musty smell rose up from the basement, Loretta strapped on her galoshes and went to check for flooding. Again, for the third time this season, sewage had backed up through the floor drain and collected on the basement floor. She poured bleach into it and told Shadrack to scoop up the excrement and mop the floor dry.

Afterward she dressed him in a second-hand suit from the Thrift Store. She dabbed her palms with Blue Magic and smeared it over his face until it shined. Then she combed his bush. "Stop moving, Shadrack," she said, whumping the back of his head. Each time the hair pick snagged a patch of rough hair, Loretta gritted her teeth and snapped it through, causing Shadrack to jump in his seat. "Move again I'll pop you," she said.

"It hurts, Mama."

"Hush." Loretta popped his head. "Think I like combing this nappy head? Stop all this whining. Stop moving." When Shadrack couldn't stay still, Loretta tugged him by the collar into the kitchen. "Straightening comb," she said. "I don't have all day to fuss with this nappy stuff." Shadrack protested, but it didn't matter. Loretta heated a straightening comb on the stove burner and smeared a palmful of Blue Magic into his hair. When they smelled burnt metal, Loretta took the burning comb and eased it through his bush.

The Blue Magic sizzled and melted. Shadrack hissed loudly, flinching as the scalding liquid dripped to his scalp.

"Stop moving, doggone it." Loretta whacked his head with her free hand and applied more Blue Magic, melting it with the straightening comb and repeating the cycle. Despite Shadrack's hisses and flinches, Loretta continued this until his hair hung straight back toward the nape of his neck. "That's better," she said. "Don't mess it up."

Loretta dressed herself in an ivory-cream skirt suit with a wide-brimmed hat cocked over part of her face. She and Shadrack each ate a plate of grits then knelt before the living room sofa for prayer, awaiting the arrival of Deacon Duke Baines, who drove the Sunday van for Gethsemane Holiness Church. *Peace Be Still* hummed softly on the record player. Loretta prayed. Shadrack spent this time listening to the sound of rainwater washing through the gutters.

When Deacon Duke Baines arrived, honking twice, and then once more, Loretta grabbed their Sunday School books and a King James Bible. Shadrack held a plastic bag over his head and followed her out.

As always Shadrack sat on the front pew of the church where Loretta could watch his every move from the alto section of the choir stand. His perpetual calm and reticence—that quiet bewilderment while everyone else was joyful and singing, skipping holy dances in the aisles—this earned him beatings for being so unclean the Holy Spirit couldn't enter him.

"Suffer little children to come unto me," Reverend Shropshire said, standing at the altar that Sunday with outstretched hands. He anointed their heads with olive oil. When Shadrack didn't leap and run through the aisles like the others, Loretta stormed down to the altar and twisted his ear.

"Don't you hear the man of God talking to you?" she said. "Let the Lord use you, boy."

Reverend Shropshire palmed Shadrack's forehead and shoved it back. When he gave no indication that a feeling of exhilaration had shot through his mind or body, Loretta smacked his head and whispered, "Wait till I get you home."

When she got him home, she twisted his ear again. "You acted like you was in outer space somewhere. Let me give you something to bring you back to earth." And she tied him to a bedpost and flayed his bare backside with an extension cord.

Over time, Loretta's devotion to Gethsemane became an indefatigable obsession. Five times a week they attended church, including Thursday night choir rehearsal and all-night prayer on Friday, where everyone fell asleep at some point, but Loretta never did, and she made sure Shadrack never did either. They knelt for hours, and whenever his sleepy head sank downward toward the pew Loretta reached over and pinched his ear.

"Prayer Warrior!" the churchwomen called her. "That Loretta sure knows how to get a prayer through."

All the saints at Gethsemane went to Loretta when they had problems only prayer could fix. When Sister Milner and her children were being evicted from their home, the saints sent them to Loretta to pray over the eviction notice. When Deacon Hargrove's grandson was arrested for selling dope, everyone said he needed prayer and should go to the Prayer Warrior. And when the doctor gave up on Mother Sanders (one of the eldest women of the church) and said the only thing, in fact, she *could* do was pray, they summoned Loretta to the old woman's sickbed.

"Lord, Lord, Lord!" Loretta cried out. Her bony hands quaked before the ailing woman. "Heal this woman right now. In the name of Jesus, I command all demons of cancer to leave this body." Loretta poured olive oil into her hand and laid it to the frail woman's chest. "Get out, Satan!" she hollered. The old woman was so shaken she almost fell off the bed. Loretta thrust her oil-soaked hand back, as if snatching Lucifer himself out of the woman's bosom. "No, no, you can't stay here!"

Loretta prayed incessantly. Indeed, at any moment, she was apt to pause everything and drop to her knees. Even before she beat Shadrack, she prayed over the belts. Prayed over the broomsticks and high-heeled shoes. Prayed over the poles and extension cords, and dipped them into holy olive oil before she lashed his naked body.

In public, she accosted complete strangers, reading scripture to them and offering them prayer. Some Saturdays she boarded the eastbound Genesee Street bus waving her Bible. "Repent, ye sinners. The kingdom of God is at hand!" And she would foretell of plagues and doom if they would not heed the words of a prophet of God.

Sometimes Reverend Shropshire would invite her to deliver words of inspiration to the church, which she eagerly did. A current circumstance normally guided her testimony, as in the weeks following the crash.

"Listen, saints," she said before the congregation, fired up. "Jesus is there to keep you from slipping and falling. Like a stair railing! He's sturdy and strong through any kind of weather, any storm. Say Amen if you believe it." People in the congregation glanced around, undoubtedly wondering whether Sister Loretta had just likened the Son of the living God to a stair railing. "I don't know about you, but Jesus is my stair railing all the way up that stairway to Heaven. Hold on to him, saints! Hold on and keep climbing."

The eccentricity of her testimonies notwithstanding, Loretta had vaulted into such a state of good repute at Gethsemane that she alone became the archetype of the good and infallible Christian. The model churchwoman, in the words of Reverend Shropshire. So when the single men at Gethsemane approached her, Loretta of course gave them no time unless it was strictly for prayer and Bible study. Nothing else. Nothing more. Because as much as God wanted to elevate her in the Holy Spirit, the devil wanted just as much to pull her back down. So she was always on guard for his tricks.

Not that the men at Gethsemane were evil. Most of them were upstanding gentlemen. But she already understood that Satan attacks you where you're weak, which meant for her he would come in the form of a good-looking man. A handsome, single man who dressed well and smelled nice. Someone, that is, like Brother Maxwell Gilbert, the well-respected choirmaster and singer, with whom Loretta became the best of friends for quite some time.

3

Brother Maxwell Gilbert was a pretty gentleman—light-skinned with Jheri curls—who wore shiny suits and crocodile shoes and wallowed in the admiration of all the beautiful women at Gethsemane. They adored him, clamored after him, and any one of them would have accepted a marriage proposal without question. But in truth, he spoke with a voice so delicate—gestures and mannerisms so effeminate—people suspected he hardly liked women at all. So it was definitely news when he invited Loretta to lead a choir song when everyone knew she couldn't carry a note in her pocketbook. People grew even more suspicious when they noticed the two of them chatting after every service and saw him offering her hugs and kissing her cheek and even giving her and Shadrack rides home on occasion. None of it made sense. Because even if the rumors were *not* true—that perhaps he was merely a sensitive man who had grown up in a house full of women, say, but nevertheless had normal manly desires—why ever would he choose a plain, thin-as-a-twig woman like Loretta to be his girlfriend? Some said it was a hoax. Others said it was for show. But for Loretta, it was God answering her prayers.

In November of that year, seven months after the crash, the temperature fell below freezing, and two feet of snow fell with it. It was around this time Brother Maxwell Gilbert accepted an invitation to Thanksgiving dinner, and Loretta's spirit waxed hopeful, mostly because she knew, as every woman knew, that only the real girlfriend got a man's time on the holidays. The others had to listen to excuses. But not Loretta. Not this time. God had finally sent her a good man, a fine man, and that man chose to spend his Thanksgiving with her. But even in that ecstatic moment, she found herself unprepared for a visitor (especially one who might actually offer a marriage proposal). So she ran and replaced the bland beige curtains of the living room window with the elegant silk drapes from her bedroom, though deep down she believed there was too much ghetto on the outside of that window for the drapes on the inside of it to matter. But anyway, maybe he would like them. Maybe he would be impressed with her taste.

She said to Shadrack, "Here, help me with these walls," and passed him a rag and a bucket of soapy water, which he carried to the far wall, wiping in circles, reaching as high as he could.

"I can't go any higher," he said.

"Try harder." Loretta took a rag, slapped it onto another wall, and whirled it about. "Get a chair if you can't reach."

Afterward, she decided to move furniture around to make more room. Together she and Shadrack shimmied the floor-model television out of its square groove in the carpet, and then dragged it to the empty side of the room and set it there, catacorner. With another burst of strength, they pushed the loveseat to the opposite corner and moved the coffee table out of the way, so that when they were done rearranging things, nothing obstructed the path to the window or the view of those beautiful drapes. "That's good enough," Loretta said. "Vacuum in here while I do the kitchen. This carpet better be spotless when I get back."

Feeling as if the wall clock was ticking in double time, Loretta hurried to the kitchen where she washed all the dishes, even the clean ones in the cupboard, some of which hadn't been used in months and wouldn't be used that evening. The stovetop needed scouring, so she did it. The refrigerator needed cleaning, so she did that, too.

Later, as she changed into a slinky velour dress, she thought about how Brother Maxwell Gilbert had made her feel so good about herself when he invited her to lead that choir song. *A Mighty Fortress is Our God*. Half the time when the lead part rolled around she barely remembered the words, but Brother Maxwell Gilbert, ever the supportive friend, would be praising God and leaping up as if her faulty utterances were even preferable to the original lyrics.

Loretta applied some blush to her face and painted her nails, which had to dry while she set the dinner table and prayed over a bottle of sparkling grape juice, because Brother Maxwell Gilbert mentioned wine, but this was all she had and could afford.

Finally, when all preparations were complete, she remembered one last thing required to ensure Thanksgiving would be perfect. "Shadrack," she said, strolling back into the living room. "Today is a real special day. I need you on your best behavior."

"Yes, Mama."

"'Cause I really like Brother Gilbert. I'll be very unhappy if you mess this up."

"I won't, Mama—"

"No, I don't think you hear me, Shadrack. I know you. Sometimes you don't listen well. I can't have that today."

"I promise, Mama. I'll behave myself."

"You don't sound real sure." She narrowed her eyes. "Might have it in your mind to act a fool when Brother Gilbert gets here."

"No," Shadrack said, shaking his head. "I swear, Mama. I won't act up."

"Hmm. Well, here's what I'm gone do anyway. I'm gone give you something to think about right now so you don't even consider acting up later." Loretta sent him for the olive oil and an extension cord, and then ordered him to lie on the floor with no shirt. She anchored him with her foot and whipped his bare chest for any mischief he had planned to carry out that night.

Shortly after, Brother Maxwell Gilbert arrived.

"Say hello, Shadrack," Loretta said, dusting snow from the shoulders of the man's overcoat.

Brother Maxwell Gilbert poked out his hands like guns at Shadrack. "Hey there, cowboy," he said, and then launched into a flailing imitation of himself directing the church choir.

Shadrack giggled.

Loretta blinked without smiling. "We didn't know if you was still coming with all that snow piling up," she said, hanging the man's overcoat in the hall closet.

"It's just a little snow," Brother Maxwell Gilbert said. "Say, you ever gone fix that stair railing out there?"

"Someday," Loretta said. "God'll take care of it."

"I hear you." Brother Maxwell Gilbert rubbed his hands and drew a huge breath through his nostrils. "Boy, it smells good in here, Sister Loretta. I'm ready to eat."

At the kitchen table, Loretta said grace and served mashed potatoes, green beans, and deep-fried turkey. She poured sparkling grape juice for the adults, only water for Shadrack.

"Thought we were having wine," Brother Maxwell Gilbert said.

"Saints not supposed to drink alcohol. You know that, Brother Gilbert."

He tasted the sparkling grape juice, then smacked his lips and frowned, clearly irritated by the empty, neutered sweetness of it. "I know what church folks always say. But if I recall correct, Sister Loretta, Jesus served wine at the Last Supper. Matter of fact, he told his disciples to remember *him* when they drink it."

"That's blasphemous, Brother Gilbert. I'm surprised at you."

"Why would I blaspheme? It's in the scripture. He wouldn't have gave it to them if he didn't want them to drink it. Ain't that right, Shadrack?"

Shadrack glanced up at his mother then dug back into his food.

"Now why you guess that is, Shadrack?" Brother Maxwell Gilbert said, dragging him back into the conversation. "Why Jesus give those disciples wine?"

"I don't know," Shadrack said. He thought for a moment. "Maybe they didn't have a lot of water in the desert."

A smile formed on Brother Maxwell Gilbert's face, and he pointed at Shadrack. "There you go, Sister Loretta. They ran out of water. I didn't even think of that. See, your boy pays attention in Sunday School."

"I learned it in science class—"

"Eat your food," Loretta said. "Brother Gilbert, we ain't in the desert. We in Buffalo. Right here on Lake Erie. So you welcome to as much water and grape juice as you please. But you won't find no wine bottles here."

"Funny thing is, I'm actually colorblind because of wine," Brother Maxwell Gilbert said.

"Colorblind?" Loretta said, nibbling on a slice of turkey. "I didn't know that."

"Yeah, crazy story. When I was a baby, my mother accidentally spilled red wine all over my face. Got into my eyes and everything. Ain't seen a single color since. Except for flashes of burgundy every now and then."

"Is that a true story, Brother Gilbert?" Loretta asked.

"Most certainly is."

"So if you colorblind, how you know what burgundy look like?"

"Well, I think it's burgundy."

"Hmm. I see," Loretta said. "In any case, Brother Gilbert, like I told you, we don't drink no wine here."

"What else y'all don't do in this house?"

"I reckon you'll know by the time you leave."

The pleasure of being in Brother Maxwell Gilbert's company was evident throughout Loretta's being, and she was, suddenly, happy and healed of all her resentments. She actually grinned at Shadrack once or twice, but he had no idea how to react to it and simply coped with the confusion by pretending he didn't notice anything—that the flirtatious exchanges between his mother and her guest were too subtle for his prepubescent mind.

Nevertheless, things were different with Brother Maxwell Gilbert around. There were no more beatings or yelling, no more monitored trips to the bathroom toilet or whippings in advance of misbehaving, no more chastisements in front of the church or hours spent locked in his bedroom staring back at a gloomy window shade and four bare walls. Because now, Shadrack, like a prisoner paroled, was free to come and go as he pleased. At last, he could watch his favorite television shows again and play board games, and listen to Michael Jackson records, and even go outside and ride the new bicycle Brother Maxwell Gilbert bought him for his birthday. He and his mother's new boyfriend traversed every avenue of intrigue that lay before them. One afternoon, when it was too cool to be outside, they visited the Buffalo Museum of Science for the dinosaur exhibit, and Shadrack gazed up and marveled wide-eyed at the colossal reassembled skeleton of a brontosaurus, which filled the gallery and reached as high as the ceiling. On another occasion, when the weather was warm, they stood on the bank of the Niagara River at Goat Island, and the bellowing wind and mist from nearby Niagara Falls soaked them like a rainstorm. "Don't stand too close to the edge," Brother Maxwell Gilbert said, warning him that he could slip on the rocks and get sucked into the rapids and swept away. And then one summer day, when it was hot and humid, they drove up to Crystal Beach Park in Ontario, Canada, where Shadrack rode the Comet for the first time in his life, and felt a kindling of emotion so stirring he could hardly keep still. Now he understood church people. Life was a rollercoaster, and whenever it plunged and climbed and plunged again, you couldn't help but throw your arms in the air and scream.

"But Mama still won't let me play with other kids though," Shadrack said when he and Brother Maxwell Gilbert sat watching a group of boys play tag football at War Memorial Stadium around the corner from the house. It was the same football field O.J. Simpson used to dash across when the Buffalo Bills played their games there back in the sixties and early seventies. It was called the Rockpile now, not much bigger than a high school stadium, and only neighborhood kids played football there these days. "She said they're all going to hell someday—that I'm a follower, so I'll end up in hell right with them."

"Let your mother tell it, everybody's going to hell," Brother Maxwell Gilbert said. "Some people in this world *are* going to hell. But not everybody. And not all at the same time. You gotta learn the good ones from the bad." They watched as one of the boys threw a long pass to a receiver streaking downfield, guarded by two others. The football dropped into his arms and bobbled out before he could get control of it.

"Are you going to marry my mother, Brother Gilbert?"

"She told you to ask me that?"

"Just wondering. I wish you would. It'd be nice to have a dad like you."

"Ever met your father before, Shadrack?"

"Mama said he's dead. She won't tell me his name."

Brother Maxwell Gilbert scowled. "That's a shame," he said. "Your daddy ain't dead. I can't believe she told you that."

"You know him? Can you tell me where he is?"

"Talk to your mother about that."

"Can you ask her for me?"

"Not my place to do that."

"If y'all get married you could ask her, right?"

"That's a big 'if', Shadrack. Anyway, you too young to be thinking about that stuff."

"Too young to think about my dad?"

Brother Maxwell Gilbert popped Shadrack on the forehead. "Too young to be matchmaking grown folks," he said. "People have to know each other for years before they get married."

But over the years, Loretta grew tired of Brother Maxwell Gilbert. The femininity of his walk. The flatness of his sex drive. And all the petty annoyances in between. A frustration bred from years of dating a man who never kissed her or reached for her breasts. Sure, sex was forbidden, but temptation wasn't. Shucks, even Jesus was tempted. Where was the romance? The lust? The sinful urges that only a God could save them from? When Brother Maxwell Gilbert had no satisfactory answers to those questions, Loretta withdrew and watched him with wary eyes. Whenever he and Shadrack clowned around out back, Loretta carried linen to the clothesline and stole sidelong glances through the gaps in the hanging sheets. When he taught Shadrack how to cut his own hair, Loretta stood outside the bathroom door eavesdropping on every word. And then, when Shadrack finally grew taller and a churchwoman donated a huge box of hand-me-downs, and Shadrack asked Brother Maxwell Gilbert to help him haul it up to his bedroom, Loretta looked askance at the man and said, "Does he really need your help with that, Brother?"

But it wasn't until Loretta became convinced he was growing closer to Shadrack than to her—always asking to take him out instead of her, buying him things instead of her—that she decided she had had enough of Brother Maxwell Gilbert and that Shadrack had had enough of him too. She ended the relationship and told Shadrack his friend wouldn't be coming back, and when it seemed, on occasion, Shadrack also "spoke too tender" or "walked too cute," she ordered him to have no contact with the man ever again. "When you see him at church run the other way. You hear?"

"I thought you loved Brother Gilbert."

"I do," she said. "But he don't love *me*." Loretta grabbed hold of his shoulders. "Did he touch you, Shadrack? Tell me."

"What do you mean, Mama?"

"You know what I mean, boy." She tightened her grip and started shaking him. "Did he grab on your balls or something? Tell me now, Shadrack. Did he?"

"Never, Mama. He's nice to me."

Loretta paused and stared at him. "You saying I'm not nice?"

"I'm saying everybody's always lying on him. It's not fair."

Loretta upturned his face with a slap. "You sound like a faggot in love," she said. "You did something with him, Shadrack, didn't you? My God, what have I done?" She shot up her fists as if to strike him again, but she did not. Instead, she drew them to her eyes and cried. "You treacherous devil!" Loretta screamed. She rushed through the house splashing olive oil onto the walls and commanding demons to flee. "You pervert," she hollered. "I cast you out in the name of Jesus. You demon, go back to hell where you belong."

More literally, she meant the gloomy prison of his upstairs bedroom, which is where he went and remained.

4

Loretta Ford had always believed, even as a young girl growing up in her slow comfortable hometown of Manning, South Carolina— back when Aunt Sadie would tie her bare body to a backyard tree and whip her there—that the way of correction was to beat a child until the pole ripped blood from the skin. This was how Aunt Sadie's parents had done it and how their parents had done it before that. For generations, Loretta's family members had lived their lives in constant fear of somehow offending the person in charge, as an assault on the body with some weapon was the usual punishment. No one ever questioned it really, because people in Manning simply did what they knew to do, and what they knew was that nothing kept order in the home like the threat of violence. So when Loretta came of age and acquired a tendency to talk smart, Aunt Sadie struck her so hard it sent shock waves through the air. And when Loretta's hips grew curves and twisted when she walked, Aunt Sadie beat the sassiness out of her with a cast iron shovel. It was only when Loretta popped up pregnant at age sixteen by a married man named Henry Jackson that Aunt Sadie simply gave up and kicked her out.

"Ain't nothing more I can do for you, Loretta," Aunt Sadie said, handing her a fifty-dollar bill and a basket of fruit. "Lord knows I tried, but I can't let you curse my home. Now take this here money, but don't you ever come back."

Surprised by this eviction, Loretta found herself actually preferring the beating she thought was coming instead. The idea she had to find another place to sleep by nightfall terrified her, especially since she had no income, no car, and no idea how a young girl in Manning should go about getting her own place. "Where am I supposed to go, Auntie?"

"Shoulda thought about that before you laid with a married man. Let him take care of you."

"You'd put your own flesh and blood on the street pregnant, Auntie?"

"Don't matter what form evil come in," she said, pushing Loretta out into the hot South Carolina sunshine. "It can't stay here."

Henry Jackson worked full-time as a machinist at a textile plant in town and rented Loretta a motel room he paid for by the week, though it wasn't long before his swarthy, thickset wife unlocked the motel room door and marched in. Henry Jackson had not accompanied her, but when Loretta sat up and saw the woman, she recognized who she was—who she must have been—frowning, standing there with her hands at her hips, a short-strap purse hanging from her wrist.

"So you pregnant, huh?" the wife said, incredulous, as if Loretta's pudgy stomach was some kind of lie she was telling. "Is it Henry's?"

Loretta nodded. "Yes, ma'am."

"How old is you, girl?"

"Sixteen."

"Lord, have mercy. You ain't more than a baby yourself."

"Henry told me y'all was divorced … said he left you a long time ago."

"Honey, we aint nowhere *near* divorced," the wife said with a snake-like reel of her neck. "Where you think he be at night?"

At once, it occurred to Loretta she didn't know the answer to that simple question. For some strange, naïve reason she had never even thought to ask him. Having had no other experience with men, she hadn't detected anything incomplete about their relationship and hadn't realized that the most fundamental part of any love affair is first establishing the identities of the two people involved. Moreover, she hadn't had a clue it was even possible for a perfectly good man, a decent hard-working man such as Henry Jackson, to swear he loved one woman while yet married and living with another. "I'll just get my things," Loretta said.

The wife helped stuff Loretta's clothes into her duffel bag. "Ain't right to make you walk the street. Let me give you a ride somewhere."

"Thanks kindly, but I'll manage."

"Be truthful now. You knew me and Henry was still together."

"First I heard of it, ma'am."

The wife towed Loretta's bag over the threshold, plopping it onto the pavement outside. "Terrible how these men trick y'all young girls, and they never end up leaving their wives." She gave a look of genuine pity. "First of all, honey, it's the wives who do the leaving, not the man. If he's really divorced, it's 'cause his wife figured out he ain't no good. Not the other way around."

With no particular destination in mind, Loretta rested her head on a splintery park table beneath a magnolia tree. A raging, flaring sun scorched Manning that day, so much so that Loretta could have sworn she saw visions of the devil in the undulating waves of hot air. As midday approached, and the sun strengthened, and Loretta could find no refuge from the heat, she rose and made her way to a shelter where the manager said all guests must be out by seven each morning and back by seven each night, or risk being locked out permanently, no exceptions.

"Truth is, I got no sympathy for unwed pregnant girls like yourself," the manager said. "I'm not gone change the rules for you either. This here ain't no welfare motel. You get up early every day, you look for work, and you come back on time or you'll be sleeping out by the dumpster. Don't like it? Get a job and get the hell out. Understand?"

"Yes, sir," Loretta said meekly. "Thank you."

The manager assigned her a bunk bed in a room she shared with three chatty women whose clothes, shoes, and overnight bags all cluttered the space. At night Loretta wrapped herself in long-sleeve sweaters and hoods to protect her skin from the tickle of brownish-orange bugs that crawled through the linen. A smelly communal bathroom was just outside their room, and the stench of it filled the entire floor with an odor of urine she could never seem to get out of her stomach. And she hated that. Hated it so much she stole the janitor's mop bucket and cleaning supplies and scrubbed the toilets and floors herself. When that didn't work, and the smell lingered, she opened wide all the windows in the room, which annoyed the other women because the windows had no screens, and houseflies, to them, were even worse than bedbugs.

When scrubbing everything hadn't worked and pushing open the windows hadn't either, Loretta knelt before the bathroom toilet and vomited her dinner, trying to get rid of the nastiness in her gut. But when even *that* didn't work, and waves of urine, it seemed, crested in her stomach, she sniffed ammonia to kill her sense of smell but ended up passing out on the bathroom floor. After her roommates found her and nursed her back to consciousness, they fussed and yelled, because every pregnant woman has trouble with smells, and she was no different.

During the day while everyone else looked for work, Loretta looked for Henry Jackson. When he finally answered his phone, he agreed to meet at a McDonald's near the motel, but he never showed, and Loretta waited there for hours, desperately watching the door. When dusk fell, and a soft rain started, Loretta dialed from an outside pay phone every five minutes, hoping someone, even the man's wife, would answer and tell her whether she'd been waiting at the wrong McDonald's. But no answer. And still no sight of him. So she waited. Heart-wounded and pregnant. Even continued to wait long after she realized the father of her baby was not going to show. For her spirit lay in ruins now, and leaving that McDonald's meant giving up on Henry Jackson, something her sixteen-year-old heart was not prepared for. When all this waiting caused her to be expelled from the shelter, Loretta phoned Aunt Sadie and pleaded for one night of accommodation. But Aunt Sadie refused and advised her to contact her Uncle Cal in Buffalo and see whether he would help.

The city of Buffalo, Loretta came to learn upon her arrival by Greyhound, lay on the snowy shores of Lake Erie in the cold blue heart of western New York, seventeen miles south of Niagara Falls and a full six-hour drive from New York City. Its downtown core connected to the small Canadian town of Fort Erie, Ontario, via the Peace Bridge, which arched high over the bustling ripples of the Niagara River. Buffalo was, by all accounts, in the autumn of 1974, the very emblem of the faithful blue-collar existence. A soiled, grizzled city tired from a long day's work, but proud of it. Though New York City had rich and celebrated personalities, Buffalo had gritty self-respect, which meant something in a place of many hard days.

The autumn sky hung low the morning Loretta arrived (much lower than it ever did in Manning), steely-gray and overcast, and a creamy white fog glossed the tops of city hall and the other downtown buildings. A few inches of snow had already fallen, and the sulfurous odor of the steel mills in the south made her stomach sick again. Many of the people she met—all of whom walked and talked faster than anyone she'd known in Manning—seemed to disapprove of her polite southern ways and treated her as if she had somehow trespassed. Women with Afros, all dressed up in their glittering flared trousers and platform shoes, elbowed past her at the bus stop and sneered at her frumpish flower-print dresses and country wigs. Some of the men walked by without speaking. And this startled her each time it happened. For even though she had heard that northern men didn't always open doors for ladies, and that often they expected sex on a first date, and that when it came to poor southern girls like her they figured they could say almost anything and she'd be hooked, she never dreamed they would have the gall to walk by and say nothing at all. So in the beginning, insulted by all of this, and ashamed she couldn't hide her humble southern mannerisms from anyone, Loretta didn't socialize much. Instead, she first set about learning how to cope with winter, which in western New York was nothing short of an ordeal. An assault of lake-effect storms. Deep white fields of snow. Frigid winds so bitter and high that Loretta, despite gloves too big for her hands and boots too wide for her feet, would still feel the paralyzing prickle of frostbite, and her blistering hands would grow so numb she couldn't even hold onto her grocery bags. The snow packed as high as the windowsills and blockaded the doors, and buried cars in driveways and on the street, and it took Loretta weeks to learn how to creep across the icy pavement without plummeting cheek-first onto it.

But despite its drawbacks, this northern city of Buffalo, New York, wasn't all bad. For if Loretta liked anything in life, she liked good food, and this place had plenty of that. Indeed, the World served itself up on a platter in this town, and it didn't cost much. Everywhere Loretta went, Greek food, soul food, Puerto Rican *pasteles* and *postres*—fast food dishes so inexpensive they were almost free. Every weekend, she feasted on a large double-cheese pepperoni pizza from Leonardi's and washed it down with a purplish-red juice Buffalonians called loganberry drink. There was the Polish Villa restaurant in Cheektowaga, and the Broadway Market near Fillmore, with its *kielbasa* and cabbage and German *schnitzel*. Italian restaurants in the north. And then, in South Buffalo, a string of Irish Pubs such as Lucky Malone's that had the best shepherd's pie and draft beer in town. Loretta's growing belly was always full, and her Uncle Cal, a well-fed man himself, made sure she never went hungry from the day she first arrived until the moment Shadrack interrupted dinner, when heartburn from a plate of spicy Buffalo wings turned out to be labor pains instead.

Shadrack was a greedy infant who suckled hard at her sore, inflated breasts, so hard that Loretta rubbed hot sauce on her nipple to slow him down. The shrieking baby took more than an hour to settle down, but when Loretta offered the other clean nipple, Shadrack didn't pull so hard. Sometimes he slept with his tongue hanging out, and this irritated Loretta further. So she pricked his tongue with a needle to force it back in. Sure, Shadrack had fits and turned colors—from a very dark brown to almost red—but his tongue now stayed in his mouth when he slept.

This swarthy baby of hers, with his broad nose and dimpled cheeks, quite reminded her of Henry Jackson—so much so she could never fully erase him from her mind, and this irritated her still. Because she missed him terribly. Some days were easier. But always she missed him. And this circumstance, having birthed a baby in the absence of its father, gave Loretta the woeful wretched feeling she had made a mess of her life.

Fortunately, she had Uncle Cal, whose three-bedroom house became a permanent home to her and Shadrack free of charge. Cal even gave Shadrack his last name because no bastards were to be born in their family. In return, Loretta cooked and kept the place clean and ran a tub of bathwater when Cal returned from work each night. And when she finally fell in love—finally stopped refusing his advances—she tended to him each night in their bedroom if only to distract from those intrusive thoughts of Henry Jackson. In this way, she became the woman of her uncle's house and lived with him for over eight years.

Cal Harris, Aunt Sadie's older brother, was in his early forties and earned a decent living working at Bethlehem Steel across the Skyway in Lackawanna. Considering he had little formal education and no high school diploma, he did well for himself and took good care of Loretta and Shadrack, asking for little in return other than what Loretta was already giving him. For the first time in life, Loretta felt secure and needed. Significant, as if her presence mattered and made a difference.

Years later, however, in the summer of 1983, the closing of Bethlehem Steel brought on what seemed like the beginnings of a hundred years of grief in western New York. And when Cal had to take a lower-paying job wiping toilets at Woolworth's, everything changed. He pawned his tools, sold his spare Chevy, and moved the three of them into a one-bedroom apartment on the east side, in the Langfield Projects, where the rent was cheap and assessed according to his income.

"But Cal," Loretta protested, "Shadrack gotta have his own room." She hadn't realized what the new arrangement was until they moved in and she saw only one bedroom.

Cal hauled the last of the moving boxes into the front room and dusted off his hands. "He'll have his own bed, Loretta," he said. "Now help me unpack these boxes."

"I can't have him under me all the time. He needs his own space."

"He'll live," Cal said. "So will you."

"But why, Cal?" Loretta said. "It ain't right, and you know it."

Two minutes. It may have taken two full minutes for the sound of Cal's powerful slap to reach the hills of Allegany sixty miles away, but it must have reached that far. For the force of it lifted Loretta clear off her feet and over the moving boxes.

"'Cause I said so, Loretta, that's why. Anytime you ready to pull some weight around here, go ahead. Cooking and cleaning is fine, but we need money right now. Instead of whining about Shadrack's bedroom, figure out how to help me pay these bills."

Loretta wasn't sure when the heavy drinking started. It could have been around New Year's Eve of that year when Cal, needing to feel better about things, took her to the Golden Nugget Lounge where they met up with Big Bruce Adams, a bouncer who spent much of the night at their table guzzling whiskey and cackling about everything. Big Bruce was a great boulder of a man, an immense shoulder-hunched rock of maybe four hundred pounds or more—immovable, as though he could plant himself in the earth and just stay there. His reputation had preceded him. For ever since the .22 caliber killer had terrorized the area, randomly killing black men on the east side, some said Big Bruce secretly carried a gun. No one knew for sure, not even Cal. But everyone *did* know that Big Bruce once broke Mr. Black's collarbone with a single punch. Mr. Black was the owner of Black's Liquor Store on Jefferson Avenue. But the incident was not Big Bruce's fault. Everyone knew that too. Because he had no way of knowing, during one of their arguments, when Mr. Black reached into his jacket, exactly what it was Mr. Black was reaching for. So no one said anything to the police. The injury wasn't fatal after all. No need to interfere with a personal matter. From then on, as with most other such personal matters, people just kind of knew it, remembered it, and let it be.

But to Loretta, what felt unsettling about Big Bruce was the way he watched her when she walked by, staring at her movements from behind a curl of cigar smoke. She felt naked in his presence and found herself constantly checking her blouse and pulling her shawl over her bare shoulders. Big Bruce offered her champagne each time Cal stepped out of earshot. But she politely declined, knowing well that no honor existed among men when it came to women.

While Cal and Big Bruce were putting back double shots of Jack Daniel's and laughing up a storm, Loretta studied all the dressed up people carousing under the gleam of strobe lights. She wondered whether it was impolite to watch as a woman across the room massaged her man's bulge under the table. Amid the bumping music, the dancing, the suffocating scent of smoke-filled air, Loretta fought against the feeling of being an imposter. She had never been a drinker. Understood nothing about dancing. And so while everyone else had apparently discovered what it meant to be happy in life, Loretta sat tapping the rim of her lonely glass of orange juice, feeling a tad sleepy and a little unsure what to do with herself.

"Nineteen eighty-four is gone be my year," Cal said, shouting over the music. This brought Loretta's attention back to their table. "It's rough out here. Reagan ain't happy unless we standing in line for that free cheese. But I feel it all coming together. Y'all hear me?"

"What you feel is that Jack Daniel's," Loretta said. "Slow down some, Cal."

"He talking crazy right, Loretta?" Big Bruce said, his voice pursy and deep. His words were slurring as well. "Cal, your life messed up like mine. Get used to it. Won't be no better after midnight."

"It's gotta get better, Bruce. 'Cause I ain't standing in nobody's cheese line. I'm not saying the new year is gone bring good times. I'm just saying, with everything I been through these past twelve months—all this bad luck I been having—shit, I'm happy as hell to wave goodbye to nineteen eighty-three."

"Well, all right, brother. I'm down with that." The rims of their glasses kissed over the table.

When the DJ put on *Wanna Be Startin Somethin,* Big Bruce shouted out, "That's my jam. Come on, Loretta. Let's dance."

"No, not me," Loretta said. "No, sir."

"Go ahead," Cal said. "Dance. What you scared of?"

"Cal, you know I ain't going out there."

"I won't bite you, Loretta," Big Bruce said. "Come on." Like some prehistoric human, he dragged her to the dance floor, wedging their waistlines together, his penis hardening against her as she wriggled and wrenched her body trying to scoot away.

Cal bounced in his seat, guffawing, spanking his knee.

When a slow Marvin Gaye song came on, Cal tapped Big Bruce's arm and handed him a drink. "I got it from here, Bruce." Cal stepped into the dance with Loretta and wiped her cheeks with his calloused fingertips. "I wanted you to have a good time," he said. "You been sad lately. Thought you needed a night out. You know I love you, right?"

"You still drunk?" Loretta said, whimpering.

"I never was, baby."

"Then you must be plain stupid letting him touch on me like that."

"I wouldn't let nobody hurt you. That's just Bruce."

"Cal, I don't want your buddies touching on me."

"That's cool, baby." He pulled her close and kissed her. "Let's dance. The new year is about to come in."

Right there, swaying in a quiet, romantic enclave of their own, unmindful of the celebration erupting around them, they slow-danced, embracing each other as the sweet-tasting hope of a better life poured out before them at the stroke of midnight.

But Cal Harris was a gambling man whose addiction to losing money became legendary on the east side of Buffalo—prone to squander an entire week's earnings in one night if the opportunity presented itself. All the while, Loretta was repeatedly begging him to stop, tearfully warning him they could end up on the street someday. She wouldn't give him a moment of peace, not even when he went to relieve himself. Once, when he was on the toilet, groaning and straining, smelling up the apartment, he finally lost his patience.

"Dammit, Loretta, stop bugging me," Cal said. "Can't a man gamble if he want?"

Loretta fired back from the other side of the bathroom door, "Gambling ain't the issue, Cal. It's the losing I have a problem with." Then she threatened to pour out all his liquor, and he threatened to do something awful if she did. And they argued back and forth this way until he swung open the bathroom door and silenced her with a couple of backhand slaps to her mouth.

One Saturday evening, Big Bruce and two other friends, Ted and Peanut, came over with plenty to drink. They set up a square card table in the front room and gambled all night. Loretta stayed up with them, gathering their whiskey bottles and cigarette butts. She served leftover catfish stew with some cornbread when they were hungry.

As it happened, Cal lost badly that night, and by extension, so did Loretta.

Barely awake, she was at the kitchen sink washing their dishes when she heard them wrangling over something in the front room. At first, she didn't pay much attention. They had been drinking too much liquor for anything they said to be worth listening to. When she finally turned to see the commotion, she saw Ted and Peanut standing between Cal and Big Bruce.

"Hey, that's enough, y'all," Peanut said, driving Cal back.

"Settle down," Ted said, holding off Big Bruce.

Cal whacked Peanut's hand out of the way and stepped into the kitchen.

"I thought y'all was friends," Loretta said, drying a plate. "Sounds like y'all gone kill each other."

"Hey baby, listen," Cal said, quietly. "I'm short a few dollars. Help me out."

"Short how much?" Loretta peeked over his shoulder at the three other men. They had settled into their seats again, and only Big Bruce had any interest in her conversation with Cal.

"Like two-fifty. You got it?"

"Two hundred and fifty dollars? Cal, you know I don't have that kind of money. Why would you even ask me? I told you to stop this gambling."

"Baby, I know you got money saved up. Where is it?"

"I had to buy some stuff. Tell Bruce he'll get it later."

"He don't want it later. He want it now. Besides, I can't let him leave without winning my money back."

"You not hearing me, Cal. I don't have it."

Cal bit his knuckle. "God dammit, Loretta. Why you spend all that money?"

"How was I to know you was gone need it?"

"'Cause I be gambling, Loretta. You probably did it on purpose to punish me."

"The money's gone, Cal. What you want me to say? I don't have it."

Big Bruce called out from the front room, "Hey now, I ain't got all night."

"Just *wait* a damn minute," Cal shouted back. Then he said to Loretta, "All right, you gone have to help me with this." He drew close to her ear. "I need you take Bruce in the back and let him fuck you real quick. That way he'll give us a break on that money."

Loretta's hands went motionless in the water. Rotten, whiskey-smelling breath reeked only inches from her face. "What did you say?"

"It's only one time, baby. I need you to do this."

"Have you lost your mind? I'm not letting that man touch me—"

"It's just this once—"

"What *am* I to you, Cal?"

"Loretta, ain't no time for this. I've been good to you, girl. Whenever you needed me I been right here. We can talk later. But at the moment, I need you to do what I asked. Now if you rather suck his dick or whatever, that's fine. I don't care. Just do *something*, but hurry up."

Loretta shook her head in disbelief, because apparently she had long been in love with a man who didn't exist. A mirage of a man presented in full gleaming Technicolor merely to facilitate the dark purpose of the scoundrel behind the mask. The provider she had come to love was a lousy pimp trying to pawn her off for the night. After all these years and all these struggles, how could he not be broken by the thought of her making love to someone else? And that alone erased all the flowers. All the long kisses. The wiping away of tears. Sounds of him declaring *I love you, Loretta. I'll take care of you, baby.* Everything vanished in that instant and could never come back. "Get outta my face, Cal," she said. "You scaring me." His whiskey breath reeked and made her sick.

"Loretta, listen to me—"

"I said get outta my face. Leave me alone."

"I'm gone ask you one more time—"

"And I'm gone *tell* you one more time, get outta my face before I have the police drag your drunk ass out that door." Loretta sucked her teeth. "Must be crazy." She started back washing dishes. "Tell you what, Cal, how about *you* go out there and suck his dick … buy yourself some time to come up with that money."

Before she even felt the force of his hand, her face was already submerged, and her next breath inhaled dishwater instead of air. Her first thought was Shadrack, and then, how the hell was she going to get her face out of that water. Each time she thrashed her way up, Cal forced her back under. Life said reach for a knife, but her desperate hands knocked over the dish rack before she could grab one.

"What, you gone kill me?" she heard him say. Then she heard, "Bruce."

Footsteps rushed from the card table to the kitchen. Peanut hollered out from the front room, "Y'all gone hurt that girl, Cal. Don't do that."

By the time Loretta's face resurfaced, Big Bruce had landed upon her from behind. Cal restrained her by her soaking hair so she couldn't flee, and about all she could do, as she remained pressed over the troubled dishwater, was empty her lungs with heaves and gags, simply trying to utter the words, "*Please stop*."

Loretta didn't leave her bed for days after that, and though the bruises had started to heal, the depression only grew worse, and she would have stayed there forever had Cal not come home one day and tossed five crisp one hundred dollar bills onto her pillow. "That's the money I owed you," he said. "For helping me with Bruce." And that caused her to get up.

"Where are we going, Mama?" Shadrack said as they walked the streets of the east side that night, Loretta striding quickly, tugging at his arm like a leash. It was March, and there was still snow. Shadrack walked without proper boots because he and Loretta had left in a hurry and could only take his sneakers.

"Shut up and let me think," Loretta said. "Move faster."

They roamed the streets for hours that night until they reached the Fruit Belt and happened upon Gethsemane Holiness Church, a grand, white-brick edifice with tall white stairs and stained-glass windows. Assembled in the chapel for an all-night prayer service was a small group of churchwomen who welcomed Loretta and Shadrack with warm-hearted hugs and prayed with them and signed the cross on their foreheads with olive oil. When Loretta sobbed in their arms, they rubbed her back and told her God would heal the pain. All she had to do was believe.

"I believe it," Loretta said, weeping. "I believe it," she said once more, blubbering now into the palms of her hands. And just like that, she was born again. She was one of them. They called themselves saints, and she was one, too. Not some aimless woman tramping through the streets of Buffalo. She had a purpose, and that purpose was to serve God. The churchwomen celebrated with her. One went to the organ, and everyone sang a song titled *I've got a new life in Jesus,* and then another song titled *Blessed be the name of the Lord,* and then another called *I'm on the Lord's side, and it makes me mighty happy.* They did holy dances in the aisles and clapped their hands to a relentless pulse of gospel swing. The organ music ignited their feet, and they stomped so hard the floor trembled beneath them. This they did until the early hours of the next morning. By this time one of the elderly mothers of the church had compassion on Loretta and Shadrack and insisted they come live with her. She was Mattie Turnbull, the one everyone called Deacon Turnbull's wife even though Deacon Turnbull himself was dead now seventeen years.

"Come stay with me," Mattie Turnbull said. "Got a beautiful house over on Peach Street. Number ninety-nine. Prettiest little garden you ever saw."

In the backyard of Mattie Turnbull's house, an old ivy-covered yew tree overlooked the grave of her dead husband. It wasn't so splendid anymore, nor well kept, because it had been the dead man's favorite tree, and Mattie Turnbull believed that a dead man's passions, and anything he might have loved more than her, should go ahead and perish right with him. Instead, her passion was a glorious sugar maple out front. It stood at the curb, alive and full, and gave shade to the steep gable of her blue and white house. Each Saturday morning, when the weather blazed hot and dry, she went out and watered its soil, then chatted with it and cut away the weeds from the mulch. When autumn came and its leaves turned red orange, the old woman sat out on the front porch and simply admired it. The flourishing flower garden of the front resembled nothing of the haunted, tangled mess in the back, which for years had been ravaged by weeds and neglect. Rather it shone as a vibrant landscape, luxuriant, sweet with the smell of roses and lilacs, violets and lilies. Bright green blades of grass cropped and mown like the plush lawn of a palace courtyard. And there pulsed a rhythm to the beauty of it. One that never died. And it gave a spurt of life to its caretaker like the beat of her own heart.

Mattie Turnbull was in her mid-eighties with a quick mind but a slow body and appreciated the company of a young woman like Loretta. It was an ideal union, actually, because Loretta needed work but had no experience, and Mattie Turnbull needed help but had no family. So Loretta did the cooking and cleaning, much the way she had done with Cal. Ran errands and paid bills. Cashed the woman's Social Security checks each month. Bathed her body and coiffed her hair. Even wiped her soiled bottom at the toilet when she needed it. In exchange, Mattie Turnbull taught her how to arrange things around the house and how to maintain a lovely flower garden even in the gloomiest part of the ghetto. And then at night, swaying in her rocking chair, sipping hot chocolate, the old woman told tales of Mobile, Alabama, and dismissed Loretta's petty troubles in Manning.

"Honey, it ain't that bad," Mattie Turnbull would insist, smelling of eucalyptus oil, teasing Loretta for not understanding how a woman could love a man so much she hated him. "Ain't no understanding it, Loretta. All you can do is live." When Loretta looked puzzled, Mattie Turnbull chortled and said, "As God is my witness, I loved that Deacon Turnbull fifty-two years and hated him at the same time. Mistreated me so bad, I couldn't tell you the half. But you know what? I kept on living. Far as I'm concerned, whoever lives longest wins. All them men who did you wrong, they'll be dead and gone someday, laying in they grave like Deacon Turnbull back there. Just keep on living."

Within those quiet walls, the drone of old-time gospel music remained the soundtrack to their melancholy lives. The bluesy warbles of Mahalia Jackson and James Cleveland made every day, every breathing moment, feel as if a never-ending prayer-service was going on at 99 Peach Street. They attended church almost every day. Prayed and spoke in tongues on the altar. Returned home again and prayed without end, splashing olive oil onto the walls and furniture to bless the house. Mattie Turnbull trained Loretta how to live like a Christian woman and how to spurn any man who wasn't her husband and how to resist the devil and all his imps, and then, most important, she taught her how to be a firm disciplinarian when it came to Shadrack.

"Honey, you gotta be hard on a boy," Mattie Turnbull said, holding out her cane for Loretta to take. "Either beat him now or one day the police gone have to do it. It's in the Bible. Thou shalt beat him with the rod and deliver his soul from hell." She raised up a trembling fist. "You gotta beat him, Loretta."

And that is what Loretta did under the watchful, cold-blooded gaze of Mattie Turnbull. She beat Shadrack for every transgression, big or small, and tied him to bedposts and trees, choked his throat, and cuffed his face whenever he did something contrary to the rules of the house. She whipped him with a pole, and extension cords, and bruised his head with a hard-sole shoe.

"You gotta *beat* him, girl."

And Loretta would beat him some more. Flung him against the wall and kicked him like a mongrel dog. Burned him with the straightening comb and chucked boiling soup onto his legs when he didn't hear something she said.

"You can't be soft with a boy," Mattie Turnbull said. "Lord knows, if I had more strength in my limbs I'd beat on him myself."

When Loretta had beaten him enough for both of them, Mattie Turnbull took back her cane and said, "Now you gotta lock him away. Put him in his room and don't let him out. 'Cause that's what the police gone do if you don't. Lock him up, Loretta, until he forget who he is and become what he supposed to be. Respectful, obedient, and silent."

And Loretta would drag Shadrack upstairs and dump him onto the hardwood floor of his bedroom. Drop down the window shade so he couldn't see out, and then slam the door behind her when she left.

"Let me explain," Mattie Turnbull said. "He seem real innocent right now. But when he grow up, everything change. He'll become a thief. Steal a woman's happiness. Make her a slave in her own home. Then have the nerve to demand loyalty when he ain't loyal. Faithfulness when he ain't never been faithful. Deacon Turnbull used to beat me with this very same cane—"

"That same one?" Loretta said.

"Yeah, this same one here. But it's perfectly all right when you use it on a child. 'Cause you training him. You learning him how to respect a woman when he get older, something most black men don't know how to do, which is why most of them end up good for nothing. I'll tell you why. See, all anybody really has in this world, Loretta, is a mind, a body, and a family. But a black man toy with your mind, abuse your body, and couldn't care less what happen to his family. That make him good for nothing. Matter of fact, the only thing good about him is that he don't live long. That's why I say keep on living.

"See, the day Deacon Turnbull died, I watched him. He wanted help, and I could sense he wanted one last chance to make his soul right. To ask forgiveness for all the hurt. All the humiliation. But I didn't give it to him. When he cried his heaviest tears, I spat in his face, knowing full well that a soul that dies without redemption is a most unfortunate one. They never sleep. Forever cry out to this side of eternity for that forgiveness. Sometimes it's late at night, and I can hear Deacon Turnbull's soul whispering to me in the dark. *Forgive me for it, Mattie. I didn't know.* But I don't forgive him. I go out to that backyard garden, under that yew tree, and spit again."

Months later, when Loretta found Mattie Turnbull prostrate on the bathroom floor, she and Shadrack became residents of a dead woman's house, and the owners of it by default. No relative came forth to claim the property, and no one at Gethsemane begrudged Loretta the inheritance. They loved her and approved of her good fortune, claiming it was only right she should have it. They buried Mattie Turnbull next to her husband in the backyard. It was brisk that morning when they carried her out, each pallbearer's pleated cuffs drenched by the snow. Loretta and Shadrack stood among a handful of church members who gathered by the yew tree singing a song of farewell to the woman they knew as Deacon Turnbull's wife. Loretta clenched at the warmth in Reverend Shropshire's arm as he committed the body to the ground.

"Father God," Reverend Shropshire said in prayer, "as we depart from this sacred garden of remembrance, watch over these souls that remain here. Even now in the hour of death, let them be blessed, and we will always give your name praise. In the name of the Father, the Son, and the Holy Ghost. Amen."

From then on, Loretta assumed the role as owner of the house at 99 Peach Street. She tended the property. Kept the house tidy. Even rocked herself in Mattie Turnbull's chair as if it were her own. When utility bills came, she used the dead woman's bank account to pay them. Telemarketers called, and she mimicked Mattie Turnbull's voice. How simple and sweet the deal. For a mere two short years of loyalty to an old widow, Loretta stood to reap a lifetime of security and independence, a measure of self-rule she had never known before, and only now began to fully appreciate.

Before long though, the bank account dwindled. This compelled her to seek real employment for the first time in her life. For months, her minimum-wage job at Super Duper yielded enough to get by, but just barely. And when hard times came, and heartbreak came, so too did a flood of Manning, South Carolina—a swell of sorrow so massive she could not escape it in any direction. This sadness—the kind a scared unmarried woman suffers when she searches for love everywhere but all she can find is sex; the kind she endures when she offers her heart but the only thing a man offers back is the buckle of his belt—this had all been warded off by the presence of Mattie Turnbull. But she was no longer there, and Loretta was no longer fortified against the abuses of her past. So naturally, in her most despairing moments, when she felt more vulnerable and empty than ever, slick men crept into the void and took advantage. One after the other, each of them masqueraded as the rescuer, and because she needed to believe them, she simply did. Believed them all, even as they cudgeled and spiked her heart with no mercy.

Then one night when she had had enough, she lay awake. For a long time sleep eluded her. Even in the dark stillness of her bedroom, she could find it nowhere. So she wept. Not because she was tired but because her heart was. Crushed by the realization that her quest for love was but a forlorn hope and that nothing in

her life would ever change. She would never belong to anyone—
never come close to being someone's wife. And all at once, that
plain old human desire to be loved was gone, like a breath in the
air, and so was her will to live.

It came to her in a vision: *A baptism. The only way to cleanse
herself and end the suffering. She stands in the doorway of Shadrack's
bedroom in a lavender nightgown. The hallway light brightens his
shadowy bedroom as he sleeps. Softly she calls out to him in the dark.
"Shadrack," she whispers, though she has to call him again before his
body stirs a little.*

"Where are we going, Mama?" he asks, walking toward her.

*"Home," she replies and removes his pajamas. His body is bare as
they proceed to the bathtub where she runs cold water to the rim so
that it overflows when they both slide in. The back of Shadrack's head
rests against her bosom. She anoints him with olive oil and pours the
rest of it into the water. She wraps her arms around his chest, her legs
around his legs like shackles, and prays, and then plunges the two of
them backward into the water never to surface again.*

It was time now. Loretta was ready. She and Shadrack were
going home by way of a baptism. Purified for all eternity. Stripped
of this miserable shell of existence. An abstersion most welcome
and long overdue. So as she pushed open his bedroom door, her
mind was already set. Her son was so young, but she had no
choice. It had come in a vision and made perfect sense. And on that
rainy Friday night in April, in the spring of 1987, she would
have done it for sure, would have baptized them both had it not
been for the noise of the crash. The suddenness of the impact
frightened her even more than her own decision to die. And now
being confronted with the reality that someone or something down
below required her immediate attention, about all she could think
to do, at least for that night, was do what Mattie Turnbull told
her, and that was to keep on living.

5

South Buffalo. The Old First Ward. Never the friendliest territory for his father politically. The only ward he ever lost in his mayoral elections, and he always lost there by huge margins. So when compelled to meet with Police Chief Douglass Gallagher at Murray's Irish Pub over on Hamburg Street, out by the jaded grain elevators that ranged along the banks of the Buffalo River, his father showed no enthusiasm, but the matter needed to be settled quickly, and this was the only place Chief Gallagher would agree to meet at this hour, somewhere close to his own home. Moreover, his father, Cornelius, had insisted on privacy, and Chief Gallagher said Murray's would be such a place. He knew the owner, an Irish American gentleman whose family line stretched back to the earliest residents of the First Ward when Buffalo first incorporated in 1832. Above all, the man minded his own business and had the useful habit of not remembering at daytime who might have held a private meeting at his establishment the night before.

Cornelius and Audwin arrived at 3:45 a.m. Last call. Chief Gallagher was sitting at the bar, slurping at the frothy head of a glass of beer, his pale, plump face rough with stubble. He was a broad-shouldered man, large-bellied. Not overly big the way a fat man is big, but strongman big, only with too much fat at the gut. This was his father's best friend. His longtime confidant, who had been his college roommate years ago at UB and had helped him orchestrate a formidable campaign during the mayoral election of 1980, and then again in 1984. His wife, Margaret, was good friends with Bernadine, and the two families were so close that the Gallagher children—two teenage daughters and a son—were like siblings to Audwin and his younger sister, Giselle.

"Margaret threatened to divorce me, thanks to you," Chief Gallagher said when he saw Cornelius. "She didn't like me getting out of bed at three in the morning and not being able to tell her why."

Without removing his trench coat, Cornelius sidled onto the bar stool next to him and signaled for a beer. Audwin sat to the left of his father, likewise keeping his jacket on, the one with the collar turned up. The rest of the pub had emptied out except for an elderly straggler who crooned a maudlin song of his beloved Ireland as he shot a final game of pool before leaving and taking his song with him.

"Anything for the young fellow?" the bartender said.

"No," Cornelius said. He stared at Audwin. "He's only seventeen. He's not supposed to be drinking. Not here or anywhere else."

Was this a joke? His father had never objected to him having beer. Sure, with his stomach still queasy, he had no taste for alcohol at the moment, but everyone knew that he, Audwin, even at seventeen, could name more liquors than anyone who dared to wager on it, and that included his father. Besides, seventeen wasn't so young anymore. Most boys his age were consuming far worse substances than draft beer and liquor. In case the *Howdy Doody* generation hadn't noticed, the age of youthful innocence had passed. These were the days of rap and sexy videos, gory horror flicks and people saying the word *bitch* on network TV. Sure, at that one instant, that one moment in time, he didn't want anything to drink, but that was no reason for his father to get in the way of it.

When the bartender stepped out of earshot, Cornelius turned back to Chief Gallagher. "Audwin had an accident tonight," he said. "Rammed into a woman's house in the Fruit Belt a little while ago."

Chief Gallagher looked past Cornelius over at Audwin. "You okay?"

"He's fine," Cornelius said. "The car's banged up, but he's fine."

"Was he drunk?"

"No. Just being reckless and stupid as always."

"It was an accident, Father—"

"Quiet, Audwin," Cornelius said, holding up his hand. "I'll talk. You sit there and keep your mouth shut."

"You're acting like I did this on purpose."

"I said shut it. Don't tick me off any more than I already am."

"It was an accident," Audwin muttered. He pouted and withdrew from the exchange. Had it been sweet little Giselle sitting there instead, everything would be different. The tone of voice. The words themselves. The level of frustration over a simple car accident that took no one's life (so what was the big deal?). His father's darling wouldn't have had to endure this. She was Giselle. She was special. He was Audwin. He would have to get over it. On occasion, his friends liked to inquire as to how it felt to be the mayor's son. He usually shrugged and offered no answer. But deep down he wanted to say it was hell, especially on a night like this. That it was unfair. All of this scrutiny and reproach when he himself had never asked for anyone's vote, had never petitioned to be on any ballot or party ticket. Yet he (and every fault of his) was always on display, embarrassed and exposed like some naked fool shivering in the street, covering his balls with his hands. But not Giselle. People had a way of understanding when it came to her. She didn't drive, so she wouldn't crash a car. But whenever she got caught in the back seat of one, half naked, making out with some upperclassman after school, the world kept spinning. Father kept smiling and forgiving. That's what he wanted to tell his friends it felt like to be the mayor's son.

"What'd the officers on the scene say?" Chief Gallagher said.

"Nobody called the police. Not yet, anyway."

"Nobody reported the accident?"

"Guess the last thing those hoodlums in the Fruit Belt want is a bunch of police dogs sniffing around the neighborhood—which is good for us, at least for now. But I don't know about this woman. There's something odd about her. I'm worried she might come forward and embellish things. We don't need that kind of press right now. Party leaders are already panicking about the poll numbers. I need you to help hold off any investigations for now—any overzealous officers, media folks with questions, stuff like that."

Chief Gallagher blushed and quaffed down the rest of his beer in one go, belching as the bitter wash tanked in his protuberant belly. "Well, nobody's above the law," he said. "I tell my officers that all the time."

"It's not about the law this time, Doug. It's about the future. Our families. Our kids. If I go down—if I lose this election—everybody goes down with me. We all lose."

The bartender checked whether Chief Gallagher wanted another beer. He said no and shooed him away. "This isn't a game, Cornelius. The police chief can't go around covering up stuff. Just let it come out. Even if it costs a couple of points or so, it won't cost you the whole election." He sighed, then added, "But a cover-up *will* cost you the election."

"I can't take that chance, Doug. These polls aren't lying. We're slipping. I'm not about to let some jackass from the city council use this against us. We've got to kill this thing."

One would have thought Audwin had set fire to the woman's house on Peach Street, or that he himself had invented the idea of car accidents when in fact they happened all the time. Why was this one different? No one could prove he was drunk. A splitting head and queasy stomach were not proof. And that Fruit Belt lady would be easy enough to deal with. Just dial up some folks, work some magic, and call it a night. The important question was what they were going to do about his car. That issue was being drowned out by the monotony of this political mumbo jumbo. His father's greatest gift to the world. Expounding at length on shit that didn't matter when people wanted to talk about something else.

"I don't like where this is going," Chief Gallagher said.

"Well, it's a whole lot better than the alternative."

"And when the media finds out?"

"They won't."

"They always find out."

"You handle your side. I'll handle mine. The media won't have anything."

"Can't do it. Much as I respect you, I can't. All I care about is doing my job and taking care of my family. I don't wanna get involved in dirty politics."

"Neither do I, God damn it," Cornelius said, speaking too loudly. He lowered his voice. "Think I like roaming around Buffalo in the middle of the night sorting this crap out? Absolutely not. But this is the hand we've been dealt, and we can't screw it up. Because I, for one, don't want to lose and watch a bunch of union bosses and liberals drive this whole damn city into the ground, and you shouldn't either. You're a good man, Doug. I'm not asking you to break the law. I wouldn't dare do that. I'm just asking you to do nothing."

And there he was. Mayor Cornelius Brooks. Not even the pretense of virtue. Where were the principles and ethics he preached about at home, the divine fatherly posture that gave him the right to moralize at times like these? He'd be lucky not to be dragged from City Hall in handcuffs if this got out. Yet somehow, a harmless, innocent car accident was worthy of beheading. Of course Audwin had always known his father wasn't perfect, that he had a slick side to him. Any son could accept that. But this was the face of a creature long hidden from daylight. The face of someone now willing to tell lies and pay bribes to win elections—someone for whom politics had apparently become blood sport: the ruthless pastime of a man who could not be killed, even by a thousand knives. Moreover, something had undoubtedly convinced him along the way that a politician couldn't afford honesty, but required a hardhearted deceitfulness, the spiteful nerves of a devil resolved to burn the world to ashes rather than let the good people have it, a cruel determination to embrace a friend only to shank him in the back on the wraparound. When had Mayor Cornelius Brooks become this man?

He must have been wondering the same thing about himself that night, sitting in Murray's Irish Pub trying to negotiate where the boundaries of loyalty lay. Trying to ascertain whether his old friend would have his back as usual, and dismiss any inquiry into an accident involving the mayor's son—curb any talk of him possibly being drunk when it happened.

6

It was a few months after the crash on Peach Street when Bernadine
Brooks, after learning that her fifteen-year-old daughter, Giselle, had
gotten knocked up by an upperclassman at North County High
School, decided that her two children were conspiring to ruin her
husband's reelection campaign. During a dinner party for the
mayor's forty-seventh birthday, Bernadine stepped onto the
second floor balcony of their home and let a few minutes of
solitude settle her down. The air was cool now that the sun was
setting, and tender strokes of an evening wind brushed over the
darkening treetops that canopied Middlesex Road.

The balcony, cozy and wide with an elegant limestone
balustrade, opened from the master bedroom. Bernadine kept the
sliding door closed to muffle the noise of The Jive Kruegers, a five-
piece jazz band Cornelius had hired for the party. Their rendition
of *Giant Steps* had just roused an ovation from the crowd of more
than fifty guests, and now, after three full sets of this endless
racket, Bernadine was ready for things to wrap up, especially since
she didn't fancy such gatherings anyway. Shaking hands and
slapping backs all night was Cornelius's idea of a good time, not
hers. Sure, these were mostly close friends and staff, but she still
felt intruded upon and wanted everyone to leave.

There was no reason to be celebrating. Although Cornelius didn't know about Giselle yet, he certainly knew about the mounting scandal over what Audwin did to that woman's house on Peach Street back in April. And now that there were rumors of a forthcoming *Buffalo News* article suggesting he had ordered officers not to investigate claims that Audwin was drinking that night, Bernadine was increasingly annoyed with even the sound of her husband's voice—a voice that was surprisingly silent a few minutes earlier when Councilman Mike Stinson, his opponent in the upcoming election, interrupted everything to announce a toast.

"To Cornelius Brooks!" the councilman had blurted out. "Mayor over all Buffalo." When everyone heard him, the party grew quiet. Bernadine, who was mingling in the large dining room, swung around to see who was speaking so boisterously in her home. Cornelius was in a crowded conversation with administrators from Buffalo State College. Members of his staff stepped toward the councilman, but Cornelius bridled them with a slight shake of his head.

"A man of many talents," the councilman said, "who has stared down storms of controversy much greater than what he faces now."

People glanced around. Police Chief Gallagher and his wife looked over at Cornelius.

Again, the councilman's voice soared. "A man of the people," he said. "Given to honesty even in a world of dishonest men. He is my rival in the polity—but my friend at heart." He bore his glass aloft. "I salute you, sir. May the best man win." When no one offered agreement, he gestured to Cornelius with an oblique nod of his head and said, finally, "May you have many more years, Mr. Mayor."

The room remained quiet. Perplexed guests still glanced about. The school superintendent was there with her husband. Both were clearly at a loss for what to do. When Cornelius said nothing,

Bernadine broke the silence herself. "Ladies and gentlemen," she said aloud, "I suspect the councilman wishes it were his birthday instead."

A burst of laughter restarted the celebration. Joyous calls of "hear, hear" went up. Music and chatter resumed. With a smirk, Councilman Mike Stinson saluted Bernadine. She nodded discreetly, and it was then she glared across the room at her husband and ultimately decided to take refuge on the second floor balcony.

Standing at the balustrade, staring out at the dusk, Bernadine didn't even turn around when the sliding door opened and the up-tempo swing of *Mack the Knife* swelled to full volume.

"This can't be good," Cornelius said, joining her on the balcony. He was drinking brandy and smiling. "Why are you being so antisocial? Everybody's looking for you. It's time to cut the cake."

"I lost my appetite," Bernadine said.

"Come on, don't worry about Mike Stinson. He's a clown."

"That clown embarrassed us in our own home, and you stood there."

"He embarrassed himself," Cornelius said. "You can't get bent out of shape every time somebody bad-mouths me. In case you haven't noticed, it happens a lot."

"So I guess when this article comes out I should pretend it's nothing—just folks clowning around, bad-mouthing you?"

Cornelius sipped his brandy. "I don't want to talk about that now."

"Of course you don't. They're about to cut the cake."

"You have a chip on your shoulder tonight, Bernadine?"

Below them, the front doors swung open. A white couple strolled out under the bright lights of the portico. The woman was Nina Grabowski, the mayor's chief-of-staff. Her husband, Jake, worked in Albany as an advisor to the governor and was only in Buffalo once a month and for special occasions. They waved when they spotted Bernadine and Cornelius standing at the balustrade. Jake Grabowski hollered through cupped hands, "Goodnight, Mr. Mayor. Happy birthday!" Bernadine and Cornelius politely waved back as the couple headed for their two-seater and revved away down Middlesex Road.

"We should get back to our guests," Cornelius said.

"That's your solution?"

"What do you expect me to do, Bernadine?"

"To care," she said. "Show some concern for your family's future. Do you want to lose? Is that what you want?"

"Do *you* want me to lose?"

"I want you to fix this problem. Did you see the look in that man's eyes?" she said, referring to Councilman Mike Stinson. "That's not a man who's scared he's going to lose. The public wants to hear from you. Tell them you didn't do it, Cornelius. Say something, darn it. Because if you don't—if you just sit back—it'll only get worse, and you're going to lose this election. But I promise you, love, I will not live in shame while you stumble around figuring out the right time to deal with everything. Fix this problem."

"Woman, I'm not fighting with you tonight. Let's get back in there. We'll talk after."

"Your daughter is pregnant, my love."

Cornelius's mouth fell open, but nothing came out. Bernadine reached for his glass of brandy before he dropped it. It was so typical of him to be unprepared for real life, to be stunned silent by it—to square his shoulders and clear his throat only to forget the tune. And after a full sixty seconds, when he finally uttered something, it was about as bland and vacuous as the look on his face.

"Giselle had sex?" he said.

"Yeah, well, your children have to get attention from somewhere, dear." And without waiting for him, Bernadine sashayed back downstairs to their guests, pretending to be cheerful and radiant and happy they were still there.

Later that night, around eleven o'clock, when the house was hushed, and the party was over, Bernadine rapped softly on Giselle's bedroom door and entered. She found her curled up in bed, embracing a down pillow. The air of the room was heavy with a peach fragrance, and a Madonna video was playing on MTV. When Bernadine lowered the volume, Giselle woke and sat up.

"You don't have to get up," Bernadine said. "I'm just checking to see if you're hungry. You didn't eat anything."

Still in school attire, Giselle hadn't dressed for bed yet. She had on a plaid skirt, a white blouse, and a pair of pink jelly shoes, and wore charm bracelets on her wrists and a friendship ring on each forefinger. "No, I'm not hungry, Mother," she said.

"That doesn't mean you shouldn't eat."

Giselle dropped her head back to the pillow. "Did you tell him?"

"I did," Bernadine said, nodding once. "He's coming to talk to you. How do you feel?"

"Sad."

Bernadine took a seat on the bed. She reached for her daughter's hand and rubbed it. "Don't worry, love. Everything's going to be all right."

When Cornelius appeared in the doorway and entered, his voice jarred Giselle to an upright position again. "Do you know how this makes me look?" he said. "You're getting an abortion. I won't let you ruin your life."

"I don't want to have an abortion, Father."

"Doesn't matter what you want. My decision is final."

"What about *my* decision?"

"You've made enough bad ones already," he yelled, and then paused as if to avoid blurting out something he would regret.

"Dear, how about we start over," Bernadine said. "Let's all settle down."

"Quiet, Bernadine. I am settled."

"You're angry, dear."

"Shouldn't I be?"

"Probably. But it won't do your daughter any good."

"Don't you dare tell anyone about this, Giselle," he said. "Not even Charles. You hear me? Then stay away from him."

"But he's the father—"

"There *is* no father. There's no mother and no baby. Am I making myself clear?"

She gave no answer. Bernadine still hadn't let go of her hand.

"Have I ever denied you anything, Giselle?" Cornelius said.

When Bernadine saw her daughter's bottom lip begin to quiver and tears well up in her eyes, she herself had to struggle not to be overcome. She thought of a time when Giselle talked about becoming a lawyer someday, and perhaps a politician like her father. A time when she didn't wear so much jewelry—didn't wear body sprays and designer shoes. Everything had changed so quickly. But the real tragedy (and the obvious reason she wanted this baby) was that she had wandered into an infatuation with Charles Vargas and lost her way back. The handsome upperclassman was now the only thing that interested her in life, and though the young man probably hadn't thought twice about her that day, Giselle, like any teenage girl in love, was sure to believe that a newborn baby would remedy that.

"Bernadine, I'd like to talk to her alone," Cornelius said. "Can you give us a moment?"

"Sure," Bernadine said. She rose and put a hand to his chest. "Stay calm in here, my love." When she stepped out into the corridor and shut the door, Audwin was standing against the wall, one hand in his pocket, the other holding a bottle of beer. He had always had that quiet, stealthy ability to be in your presence long before you realized he was there, and by the time you noticed him, you never knew how much he had already seen or heard.

"You know I don't want you drinking, love," Bernadine said to him.

"It's just beer, Mother," Audwin said. "How's Giselle holding up?"

"Your sister will be fine. Pray for your father."

"I hated to give you the bad news."

"You had no choice, my dear."

Audwin nodded.

The voices in the room were growing loud. Cornelius was doing most of the talking, drowning out Giselle's voice with his powerful shouts.

"Think you should go back in there?" Audwin said.

And then they heard Cornelius's voice blare through the walls. "You're not bringing a baby into this house, Giselle," he yelled. "That's final. I'm not letting ruin your life. I'd expect that from your brother, not you."

Audwin's shoulders dropped.

"He didn't mean that, love," Bernadine said.

"Really, Mother? What did he mean?"

"He's very disappointed right now."

"You know, it's always the same with him. I'm the screw-up in the family, and Giselle is innocent, even when she screws up, too."

"Nobody screwed up anything, dear."

"Well, you should have told him that when he cursed me out over that stupid car accident."

"Listen to me, love, he didn't mean it. He loves you both the same. This is a lot to deal with. Try to be understanding."

"Be understanding?" Audwin said. "My own father thinks I'm some kind of reject."

"That's not true—"

"Whatever, Mother. Believe what you want. I'm out of here."

"Audwin, where are you going this late? You've been drinking. I don't want you driving anywhere." She reached out to embrace him, but he brushed past her, spilling beer on himself. All Bernadine heard were his muted footfalls down the carpeted staircase and the thud of the front door closing behind him as he left. She listened for the sound of a car engine. Thankfully, there was none.

Many had long known from observation what Bernadine would only come to know by asking. And when she went forth with a mother's questions about the sequence of events that had led to Giselle's crisis, the answers came from many directions, and nearly everyone who had borne witness to the affair willingly helped her piece together an explanation of how Giselle had come to be with child. Teachers and administrators at North County had their stories. Giselle's friends offered even more. Audwin certainly held nothing back. And even Charles Vargas's paternal grandmother, his *abuela*, who knew more than she could explain in English, had done her best to fill in any blanks that may have been left behind by others.

Apparently, it started with Giselle cutting third period biology to watch him rehearse with the school band. Then, during fifth period global studies, when he and the other seniors were having their lunch, she would cut class again and prance through the cafeteria, hanging around his table, catching his notice, until the cafeteria monitor escorted her out and threatened to call her parents—both of whom were yet unaware she had begun to carry all types of hairbrushes and mirrors in her backpack, and wore peach body spray and lip-gloss, and brushed her hair in class and painted her nails repeatedly, until the teacher would start sniffing around the room for the source of the intoxicating scent. Sometimes after school, she would change from her uniform into miniskirts and cropped blouses, and then wait for Charles Vargas in the student parking lot, hoping to get a ride in his car.

"Why do you keep stalking me?" he supposedly said once, rolling down his car window when Giselle knocked on the glass. Two sophomores, Helen van Loren and Eunice Banks, caught the conversation as they passed. They didn't know Giselle well, they said, but they knew that the mayor was her father and that Audwin Brooks, an upperclassman, was her brother.

"I'm just keeping in touch," Giselle said. "It's hard to find you sometimes."

Charles Vargas drew on his cigarette. "A good man is always hard to find, pretty girl."

"Wanna give me a ride?" She wormed her body a little.

"What do I get out of it?"

"What would you like to get?"

This would have been the time he first took her home — over to the west side, in a Puerto Rican neighborhood — and then compromised her virginity in the dank basement of his grandmother's house. His *abuela* confessed she had no idea what they were doing down there until a loud grunt and sigh of relief abruptly ended their date. Poor Giselle had the look of a young lady who had fallen in love during that intimate moment only to discover that her new boyfriend was far less smitten — that his sudden spurt of sexual passion had nothing to do with his admiration for her as a person, but that it was, apparently, stunningly, nothing more than sex for its own sake.

According to Audwin, it was around this time he himself started hearing rumors and grew suspicious, and asked Giselle about her male friends, Charles Vargas in particular. Because she knew damn well she wasn't allowed to date, and he might have to tell. Giselle became defiant, he explained to Bernadine, and refused to tell him anything except that this connection with Charles Vargas was the most important thing in her life, and that her nosey brother and overbearing parents were not going to fuck it up.

"She didn't use that word, Audwin," Bernadine said. "Stop exaggerating."

"Honest, Mother, she did," Audwin said. "She's a different person now." Moreover, it was plainly obvious to him that Charles Vargas had unlocked something within her, and whatever it was — whatever it was called — it was wide open.

School band members told Bernadine that a music scholarship had brought Charles Vargas to North County High School. He played piano and sang, and talked about becoming a famous musician and songwriter someday. On weekends, he played weddings and funerals for extra cash. Sometimes he even sat in for nightclub gigs at the Humboldt Inn, playing Soul music with some of the older legends of the Buffalo music scene. He wrote numerous love songs. Giselle adored them all. Someone said he once sent tears cascading down her cheeks with an original ballad he composed and named after her (though everyone knew he had done the same for a freshman named Kylie Simonson). So, indeed, he was charming. No one disputed that. Probably mesmerized her with his over-spiced flattery—made fake words sound so real it didn't even matter whether he meant them or not.

But more than anything else—and this was the consensus report—Giselle flat-out admired him for his beauty. For he was, in her words, the most exquisitely handsome boy on earth. Product of a brown-skinned mother and Puerto Rican father. That harmonious blend of African, European, and Taíno blood that flowed together like a well-rehearsed trio of string instruments. Wavy black hair. Gleaming brown eyes. Who wouldn't be in love with Charles Vargas?

So ultimately it didn't matter whether he had already deflowered Kylie Simonson or Val Perkins or Shanti Clark, nor did it matter that every other girl at North County High School whirled in the rip current of this young man's charisma. None of them was pregnant with his baby, which was all that would have mattered to Giselle. Have an abortion? Not a chance. Only she had any real claim to the boy she loved, and if Bernadine knew anything at all, she knew there was no way her stubborn, strong-minded daughter would ever give that up.

"Yeah, but how do I know it's mine?" Charles Vargas was quoted as saying when he first found out. They were in his car. His half-cousin Anna Lisa and her grown boyfriend were in the back seat. Charles Vargas was sporting a chunky gold necklace with a Mercedes medallion, his head bobbing to an LL Cool J song on the radio.

"How many times have we had sex, Charles?" Giselle said.

By now, most people in their circle of acquaintances had suspicions, though Anna Lisa's grown boyfriend would later claim it was the first he had heard of it.

"That don't mean I'm the father," Charles Vargas said. "Nobody else got pregnant. How the heck are *you* pregnant? Don't try to play me for a sucker."

"Are you mad at me?" Giselle reached over and lowered the volume on the radio. "Tell me," she said. "I guess you want me to have an abortion."

He raised the volume again. "I can't afford a baby."

"Can't afford one or don't *want* one?"

"What's the difference?"

"Are you sure you're pregnant, Giselle?" Anna Lisa's grown boyfriend said, interrupting them. "Do your parents know about this?"

"Hey, stay out of this, dude," Charles Vargas said.

"Can you turn that music down please?" Giselle said. When she reached for the knob, he twisted her fingers and lowered it himself, slightly.

"Don't touch my music," he said.

"I want us to be a family, Charles."

He glanced over then turned back to the road. "Shit," he said, and pounded his palm against the steering wheel.

When the six-pound baby boy was born at Children's Hospital, Charles Vargas didn't bother to show up even though Bernadine left several messages with his *abuela* that everyone, including the mayor, was waiting for him at the hospital. Two days later, after still no word from him, Bernadine drove Giselle to his grandmother's house on the west side. The *abuela* escorted them into his bedroom unannounced with Giselle holding the swaddled baby in her arms. They found him playing on his electronic keyboard.

"*Abuela, ¿qué está pasando aquí?*" Charles Vargas said to his grandmother. "What's going on here?" He removed his headphones.

His *abuela* shrugged and stood back.

Then he said to Giselle, "I wasn't expecting anybody."

Before Giselle could speak, Bernadine stepped forward. "Young man," she said, impatiently. "In my family, it's always been a tradition for the father of a son to name that son. It's considered his great privilege to do so. So while you were here playing with your toy and my daughter was suffering through childbirth, we waited for you to come. When you didn't, you very much insulted my family and disrespected my daughter." She feigned a smile. "Now, believe me, Charles, I'm a forgiving woman. Anyone will tell you that about me. Even though you dishonored Giselle and shackled her with this enormous burden at only age fifteen, I still forgive you for it. But you should *never* expect me to stand by and let you disrespect her or my family." She signaled for Giselle to pass him the baby, and then pulled from her purse an unsigned Acknowledgement-of-Paternity form. "Nevertheless, you will not make a bastard of my grandchild." Bernadine dropped the form onto the black and white keys of his keyboard. "You *will* acknowledge your paternity—your culpability, at least— and then you *will*, according to the tradition of my family, name your son."

Charles Vargas stared cross-eyed at a fountain pen she held to his face.

"I fancy the name Eric," Bernadine said. "I think that would make a fine name for a son."

Not until the following autumn, during a televised debate between Cornelius and his opponent, Councilman Mike Stinson, did Bernadine realize her husband was going to lose the election. She would never tell him that of course, but it was obvious. He stayed on the defensive about Audwin's accident the entire time, and his fear of losing was starting to show. At this point, few had any reason to doubt the inevitable. The union leaders had mobilized a massive effort against him, calling it his *de-election* campaign, calling him Cornelius Crooks, and for more than a year now, the media had kept the scandal fresh in everyone's mind. Many of the local party leaders had switched their support. A number of his staff had already resigned. And the most credible pollsters in town were predicting a landslide defeat for the incumbent mayor.

How much Bernadine despised that woman on Peach Street. The one she never had the pleasure of meeting. The one who ran her mouth unnecessarily. Cornelius had promised to take care of everything. Even offered money for her poor little family. A shame the way people envy those who have status, rejoicing in their misery, foraging through the intimate details of their lives like rats in a gutter. That vindictive woman had ruined them. And for what, the mere pleasure of watching them fall?

It was over now. They only needed to tally the votes to confirm it. And on election night, a full nineteen months after the crash, Cornelius offered his concession. Bernadine stood at his side, wounded. For she would not be tomorrow what she had been yesterday and today: the mayor's wife of Buffalo, New York.

7

Long before Bernadine ever considered cheating on her husband, she had put family before everything else. It was all she knew, actually, because her mother, Valetta, had devoted herself to one husband and six kids, and Valetta's mother, Etta May Garrison, having had thirteen children of her own, had done the same. Divorce didn't exist, and for as long as anyone could remember, the shapely red-boned Garrison women of Memphis, Tennessee, had been known for being beautiful, loyal, and happily married. They had discovered the secret, and knew with many generations of matriarchal wisdom that a good man won't walk away from a happy home, and will never stray far from a loving, peaceful wife—not if he has any sense, that is.

"A strong family is the product of a strong woman," Valetta taught her daughters. "Love your husband. Work with him, not against him. Don't be sassy. Don't be mean. Being strong isn't about having a puffed up attitude. Any woman can do that. It's about resisting the forces that tear a family apart. Something only a strong woman can do."

Even as Valetta's eyes dimmed and went blind in her later days, she could still brag she never spent any of those days alone, even if she spent them in the dark. For after many years of marriage, her husband was still there—a very decent fellow in Memphis by the name of Archie Buford, a self-made man who earned his fortune in real estate, and together they raised six good-looking, well-mannered children: William, Charmelle, Cranston, Roger, Archie Jr., and Bernadine, the youngest and most beautiful.

After both parents had passed away, the six siblings split the money and departed to different regions of the country. William, the eldest, not knowing which way to go in life, simply went west and landed in Nevada where he married a Mexican woman who worked in a casino. Cranston left for Chicago to play jazz. Roger and Archie Jr. relocated to Nashville and founded a law firm. And Charmelle, having been accepted to law school at the State University of New York at Buffalo, took her younger sister, Bernadine, up north with her.

Though apart, the six siblings kept in touch. When some niece or nephew finished high school somewhere, everyone attended the graduation ceremony no matter how far away. If a wedding or christening or special Thanksgiving happened, they all made sure to be there. Because they were the Bufords. They were the Garrisons. And that meant they were family.

At age nineteen, not long after moving to Buffalo, Bernadine met and married Cornelius Brooks, a twenty-nine-year-old school board representative planning a run for city council. Though not immediately smitten with him (he came a tad old and dark for her taste), Bernadine found him charming and respectable and capable of arousing a person's trust with his spoken words, which was worth something in her book. So while her snobbish girlfriends turned up their noses at her choice, she chose to fall in love and figure the rest out later.

"I'm going to be mayor someday," Cornelius had said once over ice cream at Dairy Queen. "Then governor."

"How do you know that for sure?" Bernadine asked.

"I just know," he answered.

And she believed him. Trusted him. He was going somewhere, and she wanted to go there, too. But what inspired her most about him was not merely his ambition, for she had known wealthier men. Nor was it his love, because others had proclaimed the same thing. What had won her over and changed her very taste in men was his clear and surprising indifference to her beauty, as though her lovely face alone was not enough to impress a man like him—which was important, because when she spent time with Cornelius, she was smart, not just pretty; strong, not just sexy. And this set him apart. For any simpleton can admire beauty. Only a man of substance can appreciate strength. Maybe he wasn't fair-skinned and wealthy like the others, but so what? Cornelius Brooks had character, and that made up for what he didn't have. In other words, they married and had two children, Audwin and Giselle, with the initial years being cheery and well-spent.

Over time, however, Cornelius became so preoccupied with winning elections he wasn't the devoted husband and father Bernadine had expected. He spent little time with her, and even less with the children. When Audwin started having trouble in school, Cornelius, having been elected mayor by this time, rarely visited with his teachers, and when the neighbors complained that Audwin had begun to set fires in the neighborhood, Cornelius told Bernadine he would deal with it later.

"I know what that means, love," Bernadine said before he left to attend a fundraiser. She wanted to slap him. "You don't want to be bothered. So caught up in your own life you forgot about ours. Sometimes I think we'd be happier if you sold insurance or drove a bus."

"Bernadine, can you manage these kids without whining for once? I can't be in two places at once. I'm working for all of us, not just me. Get the boy some hobbies or something."

And Bernadine would bite her tongue and reminisce on things Valetta had told her.

"Keep peace in your home, daughter. Work with your husband, not against him. At the side of every successful man is a strong woman. Guess who's at the side of the man who fails."

"Everything's on the wife, Mother?" Bernadine asked once. "What about the husband? Even the Bible says the man is head of the house."

"Bible says the man is head of the *woman*," Valetta snapped. "But that a wise woman builds her house while the foolish woman tears it down. Don't be a foolish woman. Build your house. Don't tear it down. Our men need us, daughter. When we're strong, they're strong. When we're better, they're better."

The year Audwin turned thirteen, Cornelius allowed him to drink beer on Sunday afternoons while they watched Buffalo Bills games on television. Once when they were finishing off a six-pack in the den, Bernadine walked in and said, "Do you have to teach him all your bad habits, Cornelius?"

"It's no big deal, Mother."

"Audwin, shut your mouth."

"He's old enough to handle one or two," Cornelius said.

Audwin raised the beer can to his lips with a smirk.

"Audwin, put that down. You don't even like beer. Stop trying to impress your father."

"Mother, come on . . ."

"Do what I ask, please."

"Leave him alone, Bernadine. He's not hurting anybody."

"He's hurting himself."

"We're watching the game, honey."

"Fine, love. He's your problem now." And once again, she bit her tongue.

A few years later, after reelection, things worsened. Cornelius spent even less time at home, and Audwin, with his drinking, smoking, and hanging out late, rebelled so recklessly that Bernadine required Valium to stave off a nervous breakdown. It was around this time the security guard at the Market Arcade Cinema on Main

Street detained Audwin for lighting up reefers with a schoolmate during a showing of *Lethal Weapon*. The friend had gotten away, but Audwin, weed in hand, was apprehended before he could escape. Fortunately the head manager, having several sons of his own, was an understanding man.

"Mr. Mayor," he said, giddy, when Cornelius marched through the doors of the cinema lobby with Bernadine. "Gosh, I had no idea." He gave Cornelius a hearty handshake.

"Let's talk," Cornelius said, and they exchanged words in private. Afterward, during the drive home, Bernadine asked him how he had convinced the manager to drop the issue.

"I'm persuasive," Cornelius said, and neither of them said anything more.

A short time after that, a fourteen-year-old girl from across town accused Audwin of taking advantage of her. She had snuck out of the house one night to ride with him in his new car. They drank beer, she claimed, and got drunk, and then he took advantage. Audwin wouldn't stop even though she resisted, and kept taunting her with the words, "This is love, girl. This is how you love."

It sounded far-fetched to Bernadine at first, but then another girl came forth and said the same thing. Audwin had picked her up, got her drunk, and showed her what love is. But Audwin denied it all, insisting each of the girls was upset because he hadn't called again. Yes, he had said the love thing, but each girl was on top of him, riding him, when he said it. So how could he have forced them to do anything?

When Bernadine took the matter to Cornelius, he defended Audwin. "Feeling violated and actually *being* violated are two different things, Bernadine," he said. "Sometimes girls get their feelings hurt. We didn't raise our son like that."

"Oh, I didn't realize *we* were raising him, dear. Seems like I'm doing everything."

"Don't start, Bernadine."

"If he's out there forcing himself on girls, he needs help."

"All my son needs is to stop spending so much time on the east side."

And this, he told Audwin, was actually a valuable lesson. Something many have had to learn. That in the end, even if you rise to the greatest heights, you're only as good as the people you sleep with.

Nevertheless, these young girls from the east side, and their families, were greatly insulted and hurt, and when the situation became volatile and threatened to become public, Cornelius visited the parents of the offended girls, and somehow, after meeting in private, nary a soul uttered a peep about it again.

During Sunday dinner once, Audwin announced that he had become a Muslim, like Malcolm X, and wouldn't be eating any more pork. Never again to partake of any swine. The other three people at the table didn't react at first, because if Audwin didn't want any of Bernadine's honey-glazed ham, then he was simply leaving more for everyone else. Only when he grabbed hold of Giselle's wrist as she raised a fork full of ham to her mouth did Bernadine finally speak on it.

"Audwin, my dear," Bernadine said, mincing her food. "Release your sister's hand, please. She's still a Christian like us."

"Yeah, whatever," Audwin said. "I'm trying to save you all from killing yourselves."

Giselle pried her wrist free and gobbled the ham. "You're an idiot."

"Don't call your brother names, dear," Bernadine said.

"By the way," Audwin said, "I'm not going to church with you guys anymore. Only mosque from now on."

"Cornelius?" Bernadine said to her husband.

Cornelius shrugged. "What can I say? He doesn't want any swine."

A week later, Mr. Monticello, the principal at North County High School, notified Bernadine of Audwin's suspension for brandishing a switchblade in front of other students during an argument over someone's girlfriend. The school administrators hadn't seen it or found it, but they were sure not all the students were lying at once.

"Where's the knife, son?" Bernadine said during their meeting with Mr. Monticello.

"I don't have one, Mother. I swear."

"Everybody's lying on you as always," Mr. Monticello said. "Ten kids—that's twenty eyes—saw you pull out a switchblade like you were going to stab that kid. You saying everybody got it wrong?"

"Yep. They all got it wrong. I don't know what those morons think they saw—"

"Audwin, don't use that language," Bernadine said.

"I don't know what they saw, Mr. Monticello. It wasn't a knife. Maybe a pencil or something. I don't know. Or a sharp pen. But a knife? No way."

"This is serious, young man. We have a no-tolerance policy for weapons here at North County. What if you'd hurt that kid or any of the others?" Mr. Monticello scribbled something onto a paper. "I'm giving you five days suspension. That'll give you enough time to find that switchblade."

"Give me a hundred days then, 'cause I still won't have one. Can we go now, Mother?"

"Where's the weapon, love?" Bernadine said. "More important, where'd you get it from? Are you in a gang? Do you have some friends your father and I don't know about?"

"I told you, Mother, I . . . don't . . . have one."

A short while later, Audwin told Bernadine he planned to drop out of high school altogether because he didn't want teachers filling his head with lies. He needed to know his own history for himself. "See, Mother, that's what history is," he said. "*His*—story. Not mine. I need to learn *my*—story. Because that's exactly what it is. A *mystery*. Get it, Mother? It's all lies."

When Bernadine met again with Mr. Monticello, she learned that Audwin wouldn't be graduating on time anyway, and that she should consider enrolling him in an alternative GED program. When Audwin even ended up dropping out of the GED program, Bernadine insisted he apply for a job. After she helped him fill out scores of applications, he secured a position as a bus boy at the Oxford Lounge in North Buffalo. Two days later, Bernadine received a call that she needed to pick him up right away. He was hysterical, weeping face down on the manager's desk. The manager could do nothing to console him. When Bernadine asked Audwin for an explanation, he merely said, tearfully, "I can't do this, Mother."

"Then what do you want to do with your life, dear? You don't want to go school. You don't want to work. Don't want to go to the army. What do you want, son?" But as always, nothing. No answer. So she stopped asking, reasoning that she had little power to inspire the heart of a boy to become a man. It must be done by his father. But by this point, her husband was so distant and so determined to win reelection Bernadine wondered whether he thought he had any fatherly responsibilities at all.

Yet of all the things Cornelius did to disappoint her during this time, the sudden abstinence hurt most. Abruptly, and without explanation, their sex life dwindled from three times a week to none at all. Even on their anniversary night, after Bernadine sidled into bed naked smelling of raspberry bath soap, Cornelius turned away from her advances.

Her sister Charmelle had warned her this might happen, especially with an older man. "Gets weaker by the day, I'm afraid," Charmelle had said over the phone. "You don't notice until one day it doesn't move you like it used to."

"It's not that he has no vigor," Bernadine said. "He just seems, I don't know, already satisfied or something. You think he has another woman?"

"Probably," Charmelle said. "There's only two sure things in life, my sister. One is that a black man is bound to cheat at some point. I can't remember the other thing."

"So what am I supposed to do?"

"What *can* you do?"

"Get even, I guess."

Thus, when it came to Bernadine's new sexual fantasies, it wasn't that she had fallen out of love with her husband. She hadn't. But if she could get someone to caress her for a moment, even if wasn't him, she might feel better about things. For what Cornelius failed to understand was that his touch was more than an invitation to sex. It was evidence that she still mattered to him and that even after eighteen years of wedlock she was still so alluring that he couldn't possibly rest without making love to her first. So when the kissing stopped, and the touching stopped, and the flow of his desire had shut off like a spigot, Bernadine began to fantasize about the young southern doctor who visited the house that rainy Friday night in April when the accident happened.

At around 2:15 a.m., when the call came that Audwin was stranded at some woman's house on Peach Street in the Fruit Belt, a shortness of breath flew Bernadine's hand to her chest. "Lord Almighty, what happened to my son?"

"A little accident. He's all right." Cornelius dressed in a hurry. "But the car's banged up. I sent a tow truck."

"But not an ambulance?"

"No need."

"Are you insane, Cornelius?" She stepped in front of him. "Our son was in an accident. I'm glad you care what happens to the car."

"Calm down. He hit a pole or railing—something like that. It's not serious." Cornelius twirled open the wall safe and stuffed money into his pocket.

Giselle moseyed into the master bedroom barefoot, rubbing sleep from her face. "What's going on?" she said.

"Go back to your room," Cornelius said.

"Is Audwin all right?"

"Your father told you to go back," Bernadine said loudly.

Cornelius shushed Bernadine then said to Giselle, "Your brother's all right. Go back to your room."

"Fine, I'm leaving. Goodness, gracious."

"Are you taking him to the hospital or not?" Bernadine said.

"Just get a doctor over here."

"Cornelius, please—"

But he had already grabbed his trench coat and keys and left.

He was Jason Carter, a physician at Children's Hospital. Nina Grabowski arranged it when Bernadine said they needed someone trustworthy to make a late-night house call. Genial, holding a black medical bag as he stepped into the foyer, Jason Carter explained that he had been more than happy to oblige when he received the call.

"Yes, come in, Dr. Carter." Bernadine said, taking his jacket. He was a lean, slim-chested man of tawny complexion with a neat brush of stubble on his face like the man from Miami Vice. "Are you one to keep a secret?" She showed him to the family room.

"That's why I'm here, right?"

"So you understand my husband's situation?"

Jason Carter nodded.

"Good. You'll be compensated."

Courteous though he was, Jason Carter had irreverent brown eyes, and Bernadine felt them all over her body like hands. Groomed and clean, smelling of Calvin Klein, he was a man forever prepared for the presence of a woman, and his Tennessee drawl reminded her of gentlemen back home—Southern gentlemen whose enduring charm traveled with them everywhere they went in life.

"Your husband's not here?" Jason Carter asked.

"He'll be back soon." Bernadine gestured toward the bar and offered him a drink, but he declined, saying he never drank when he worked. "You'll have to forgive me," Bernadine said. "I'm not used to having visitors at this hour."

"That's all right," he said, warmly. "If it makes you feel better, I'm a little caught off-guard as well."

"Why would that make me feel better, Doctor? My son could be hurt. Are you prepared to deal with that?"

"Certainly. Provided it's minor. Anything serious and I'll have to take him to the ER. There's only so much I can do here."

"Tell that to my husband."

"But if he contacted you on his own and claims he's okay, no broken bones or pain in his neck, no major lacerations or anything, then I'd bet he's just fine. Wouldn't worry too much."

"I pray you're right. When we know that for sure, then I'll feel better."

"Whatever I can do, ma'am, I will. Would be my honor. Not often I can be of service to such a well-esteemed family." He leered. "Have to tell you though. I had no idea the mayor has such a beautiful wife."

"I see," Bernadine said. "Well, men hit on me all the time, Doctor, but not usually when my daughter's in the bedroom right above our heads."

It was no accident Bernadine saw Jason Carter again. They met in Allentown at the Freedom Café, a grungy, brick-walled haven for twenty-somethings who came there to read Karl Marx and philosophize about the meaning and politics of life. Hot buttered bagels and croissants warmed on a conveyor oven behind the counter. Jason Carter ordered tea, and a clerk with prodigious moussed hair and hoop earrings poured their beverages into ceramic mugs that had polychrome peace symbols painted on them.

"I've never been here," Bernadine said, sipping her tea. They found a table away from the main window. Other than the Indian sitar music playing on the clerk's boom box everything was rather quiet. A woman dressed in black with black hair and black lipstick sat on a velvet sofa, holding a mug in one hand and a paperback book in the other. Two men in parachute pants shuffled pieces across a vinyl chessboard.

"Figured you'd want to keep a low profile," Jason Carter said, smiling. Bernadine didn't smile back. On the wall behind Jason Carter hung a small chalkboard with a listing of the day's soups scribed in lime-green chalk. Beneath that was posted a daily discussion topic: *Is Ronald Reagan the Anti-Christ?*

"People know my husband. They don't too much recognize me." Bernadine took another sip of her tea, and they chatted about small things for a while: medical school, Buffalo's schizophrenic weather, Cornelius and the kids, Tennessee. Jason Carter had also come from a prominent family, born the only child to older parents, both of whom were doctors. Like most men back home, he exhibited a politeness that was both genuine and subtle (not slick and rude like Northern men)—a willingness to flirt and just leave it there, harmless and benign, because that's how a Southern gentleman should treat a woman.

"You into politics, too?" Jason Carter asked.

"Heavens no."

"So what interests you?"

"Other than family?" Bernadine said. "Well, I collect things sometimes. Cutlery and china mostly. Some antique furniture and quilts. You know much about these things?"

Jason Carter shook his head. "Nothing at all."

"I suppose you collect women instead."

"I didn't come up North for a woman, if that's what you're wondering."

"Maybe you make many house calls."

Jason Carter laughed at this, and as they exchanged a glance, Bernadine offered a soft grin in return. A tall man wearing a spandex mini skirt strutted into the café and paid for a coffee with coins he pinched from his leather purse. Taking a seat at one of the tables, he crossed his legs and lit a cigarette between two long fingers. He gazed out the main window, alternating between swallows of coffee and drags of the cigarette.

"This was a first for me, actually," Jason Carter said. "The house call, I mean."

"Well, in any case, I imagine you've met many young women since you've been here. Single ones."

"A few. Not many."

"My sister Charmelle is single. Maybe you'd get along with her. She'd be happy to meet a nice man."

"She beautiful like you?"

"We're sisters," Bernadine said. "But she's forty-four. Older women interest you at all?"

"They do, but forty-four is stretch." He laughed again. "So, how old are *you*?"

"I'm not single, dear."

"I wasn't propositioning you."

"I'm sure," Bernadine said. "I'll be frank, Dr. Carter, I do find you charming. But I'm afraid you're not so different from most men. You all have that one incurable defect. When you want something, you can't hide it, even if getting it depends on first exercising a little restraint . . . and of course, discretion."

"You mean can I keep a secret? I thought we already established that."

"You don't have children, dear. You don't have to weigh your decisions against other people's happiness. You simply do what pleases you. It's rare when I can do that."

"Visit me later," he said.

"I'm visiting you now, love."

"I'm off at nine. I don't live far from here."

"I only came to thank you for helping my son." Bernadine grinned again, if only to hide the uneasiness in her lungs. She would have suffocated sitting there had Jason Carter's pager not suddenly buzzed across the table and summoned him to leave. He scribbled something on a napkin and left it with her. In the car, she read the note, which gave the address for his Niagara Street apartment on the west side. Bernadine exhaled long breaths, trying to relieve herself of that breathlessness.

Around nine thirty, she veered into the parking lot of Jason Carter's low-rise apartment building. Silhouettes moved in the glowing windows of the square, three-story edifice. Jason Carter would be home by now and must be pacing the floor, wringing his hands in anticipation. Bernadine ruminated for a while. Do it and get it over with was her first inclination. Worry about the consequences later. But then she changed her mind, because she couldn't betray her family that way. Soon after that, she again decided to do it, because no one would ever know. But then she changed her mind again, because she didn't even know this man.

Back and forth she went with this, until she decided, finally, she would definitely do it, but just once. This wasn't the right thing to do, but being her husband's doormat was no better. Indeed, adultery stank in the nostrils of God. But where were the thunder and lightning when Cornelius did his dirt? And the fact still remained, if there were no need for it—if he'd been making love to her as he should, giving her the intimacy and attention she deserved—the sweet temptation of a man such as Jason Carter would have done nothing but turn her stomach and roll her eyes.

Bernadine shut off the engine and unlatched her seatbelt, then flicked on the interior light to check herself in the vanity mirror. When she reached for the door handle, her fingers stopped.

"Bernadine Buford," she said to herself (only Valetta would have said her name that way). "Are you sure about this?"

And she wasn't sure.

All over again, she began the cycle of changing her mind and changing it back. For thirty minutes, she sat with her forehead pressed to the steering wheel, her mind debating whether this handsome doctor really had the power to cure things. Something was wrong in her life, but she wasn't certain this was the answer—that Jason Carter himself was the remedy.

After an hour of nothing, Bernadine figured she might as well go home. Coming here was a dumb idea. Cornelius and the kids must be worried sick by now wondering where she went. But when she thought of her unwillingness to cheat that night, she hung her head and wept. Tears laid waste to the made up face she had prepared for Jason Carter. Yet this weeping, like an exhalation of pure air, relieved that breathlessness. So each time thereafter, whenever she felt breathless, she knew where to go. The address was scribbled on the napkin in Jason Carter's handwriting. She told her family she was going for some air and then drove to that same spot. At least three times a week she found herself parked outside his apartment building, ruining her makeup again: crying over Cornelius's sociopathic lack of remorse for rejecting her every night, or Audwin's mindless contentment with having nothing in life, or Giselle's bullheaded indifference to the hardships of a teenage pregnancy, not to mention the shame of having her virtuous young image sullied forever. All these things kept bringing her back to Jason Carter's place—to the parking lot anyway.

Bernadine hadn't bothered to explain why she never showed. She figured she'd make up for it later when she had more courage. But at this point, lying naked in the arms of someone other than her husband had become too stressful to imagine, much less carry out. And the very thought of pursing her lips to another man's flesh spewed the taste of vomit up her throat. So for months this was all she did. Parked herself outside the home of a twenty-something-year-old doctor and just let loose. It would suffice for now, although even this would be tough to explain if Cornelius found out.

"Have you lost your mind, Bernadine?" her husband might ask.

And she might reply, "I don't know, love. Perhaps I have."

She always made sure to shower first. Curled her hair nicely. Bought a new blouse if she felt like it. Put on fitted jeans sometimes. Even perfumed her bra and panties. But each time, she merely sat outside in the parking lot weeping. Wailing. Flirting with a ruthless point of no return, when only her dignity as a woman kept her from opening that car door. Cornelius had no control over it. If she wanted, she could twist right up to Jason Carter's doorbell, and only the two of them would ever know. She could go all the way with that handsome doctor, enjoy every minute of it simply to spite her husband for eighteen years of bullshit when she didn't have to marry an older man to begin with.

"Out with your boyfriend again?" Cornelius said one night when she arrived home late. She almost urinated on herself before she realized he was being cynical.

"Yes, in fact I was," she said.

"Had fun?"

"Always, love."

"Anywhere special?"

"We made it special."

"I see you bought a new handbag. How much was it?"

"Two thousand, dear."

"Dollars?"

"I like nice bags, dear."

"Then it better be a bag full of money," Cornelius said. "Because we can't afford all this spending just so you can look fabulous for your new stud." And then he laughed, as if their entire marriage was a joke.

Astounding. For only because he didn't know how close he'd come to humiliation did he have the luxury of still taking her for granted. How could he joke so fearlessly about another man? She could have another man with the snap of her fingers, and there was nothing any cynical, unarousable husband could do about it. In fact, when her affair with Jason Carter ended, it had nothing to do with Cornelius at all. It was because she saw the young doctor kissing another woman outside his apartment building. Bernadine shed no tears that night. She actually felt violated and went home. After that, she no longer perfumed her undergarments when she went out, and didn't see the need for fitted jeans. They were too darn constricting anyway. When Cornelius questioned why she no longer required so much fresh air, Bernadine paid him no attention, knowing that she had spared the foolish man. Could have destroyed him, but spared him. Selfish as he was, and smug, he assumed she would never hurt him that way, when in fact she could've broken his heart into forty-seven little pieces, one for each year of his pathetic, self-centered, egotistical life. But no, she spared him. Mercifully spared him, all because of her dignity as a woman. Damn near saved his life and he didn't know. And if he thought her steadfast devotion was proof that she was hopelessly enamored of him, he was dead wrong. Actually, it meant she was still a Garrison woman, and those women didn't ruin their families. How lucky he was to be married to one of them, one of those women everyone knew were always beautiful, loyal, and happily married.

8

According to the older residents of the Fruit Belt, The Blessed Home Funeral Parlor had once been a home for the mentally ill. A place of noises back then, when the constant sounds of gurgling and screaming were so intense one would have thought deranged minds were being raised and slaughtered in that very place. But ever since Harold Niederpruem moved in and converted it to a funeral parlor, it had become a quiet and unassuming place, as if the parlor itself had stepped back into the shadows of the street corner where it stood. It was, perhaps, because Harold Niederpruem himself was a quiet and unassuming man who forever tended to his own affairs and only spoke when something needed to be said. And aside from attending mass on Sunday mornings at the Southside Church of the Redeemer, he apparently did nothing else but work, and made the trip from Seneca Avenue in South Buffalo to Lemon Street in the Fruit Belt every day without fail. For years, his only employees were his loyal wife, Isabelle, and his obedient grandson, Nestor, who both worked just as hard and demonstrated the same passion for the business. But when Isabelle took ill and Nestor left for the Navy, Harold Niederpruem was compelled to seek help outside the family. He thus posted a help wanted sign in the front window of the parlor and hired Shadrack to be his assistant.

Shadrack was then eighteen years old and done with high school. During his junior and seniors years, he had helped his mother pay bills by working part time at the Hunt Senior Center on Locust, doing about fifteen hours of janitorial work per week. But now that high school was finished, leaving no cause for any more learning, his mother had demanded he fill his God-given extra time with regular employment and a full salary.

On the first day, before even settling on the terms of employment, he and Harold Niederpruem were already driving to a house on Maple Street for a removal. An elderly widow waited at the side door as they unloaded the gurney from the van.

"Listen, Shadrack," Harold Niederpruem said. "When you get to the door, I want you to greet the widow as politely as you can, explaining you're sorry about the death of her husband and so forth, and then offer a hug and kindly ask for the death certificate." Harold Niederpruem was a stout, balding man with a hunched back, dressed in worn shoes and a suit jacket too large for his upper body. Though his movements weren't as fluid and strong as they must have been in his younger years, there was a certain ease in the way he moved about, hoisting his end of the gurney and rolling it up the driveway. "Never, *ever*, remove a body without that death certificate, Shadrack. That understood?"

"Yes, sir," Shadrack said, and he did exactly as told. After the widow produced the death certificate, the two men rolled the gurney toward the dead man's bedroom.

"I went to make him some breakfast," the widow said, escorting them. "When I came back he wouldn't wake up. Used the bathroom on himself and everything, but I cleaned it."

The bedroom smelled of mothballs and bowel movement, and was brightened by a column of daylight that shone through a curtainless window. On the bed, covered to his waist, lay a bare-chested elderly man with his mouth partly open as if his final words were still stuck in there.

"You frighten easily, Shadrack?" Harold Niederpruem said.

"No, not really, sir."

"Good." Harold Niederpruem passed Shadrack a pair of latex gloves. "Put these on," he said. "Always wear gloves."

"I told you already I cleaned him up," the widow said.

Turning to her, Harold Niederpruem nudged the rim of his bifocals. "Yes, ma'am. A fine job you did. A very fine job."

"'Cause he don't have no disease or nothing. It was just his time to go."

"I understand, ma'am," Harold Niederpruem said. "And we're terribly sorry for your loss." He gestured for Shadrack to help him hoist the dead man onto the gurney. They strapped him in and rolled him out.

After two weeks of removals, embalmings, and funerals, Harold Niederpruem paid Shadrack his wages in cash. "You remind me of Nestor," he said. "You do your job without complaining. I like that." And so it was, every other Saturday, Harold Niederpruem compared Shadrack to his grandson and handed him a fistful of cash for his labors.

Shadrack wasn't particular about where he worked. Ultimately a living had to be made, and the most important thing was that he found a way to do it. Indeed, pure chance may have guided him past The Blessed Home the day Harold Niederpruem posted the help wanted sign, but it may as well have been Destiny as far as he was concerned. Because even if he should, on occasion, as most humans might, grow tired of the sight and stench of death, he willing endured it for the sake of work and the stability of regular pay.

Before this, Shadrack hadn't known Harold Niederpruem personally, but he had always heard certain things about him: that people liked him, and that no one bothered him even though he was the only white person who still conducted business in the neighborhood—said to be a serious man, but a selfless one, who cared about his clients and made little fuss over late payments or long-standing debts. And Shadrack, after working at his side for months, witnessed the confirmation of it all, and beheld some of the most impressive, heart-warming funerals that anyone in the Fruit Belt, living or dead, could hope to be a part of.

But what intrigued Shadrack most about this man was that although he spent nearly his entire life among the dead, he surprisingly worried so little about death. And this was one of the mysteries of Harold Niederpruem. An old man such as this, Shadrack thought—one with a bad back and a worsening cough, and aches and stiffness settling in his joints like rigor mortis, one who must surely be coming to terms with his own mortality—would naturally be tormented by visions of himself on someone else's embalming table. But it was not so. If anything, Harold Niederpruem drew inspiration and longevity from his occupation. The plans for tomorrow, it would seem (a grandmother's wake, a child's funeral, a man's burial) all sustained him for another day's work. Families were depending on him, and nothing strengthened his back like comforting them in the time of mourning.

Indeed, the idea of needing people to die so one could make a living seemed a tad scandalous to Shadrack at first. But he came to realize that no funeral parlor worker ever cherished death, only accepted the arrangement as it was. The halted heart was a dark necessity for the survival of the profession. In any case, mining gold from other people's misfortunes was quite common, as with the policeman, who, for the sake of his own relevance, needed the burglar to burgle and the killer to kill, and for both of them to be pretty good at it. So Shadrack, much like his new mentor, chose not to meditate on death too much and became immune to the stench of flesh and formaldehyde that greeted him each morning as he breached the threshold of The Blessed Home.

By this time, after saving up enough money (three hundred and fifty dollars), Shadrack bought a 1981 Citation out of a neighbor's backyard garage. Before long, he found himself cruising through every quarter of town. Some evenings, he visited the marina and listened to the screeching seagulls that soared out over Lake Erie. Other times, he circled the city limits, exploring the suburbs of Cheektowaga, Amherst, and Williamsville, often forgetting how he got there and how to get back. He even ventured far south into the hills of Allegany County, along the Genesee River, where purplish sunsets spread out like Heaven over the valley towns and mountains, and unfolded before him the splendor of a world he never knew existed.

But having a car also meant being on standby whenever his mother needed to go somewhere. When his excursions kept interfering with this, Loretta demanded that he leave his keys with her. "You act like that car is more important than me," she said. "What's more important than your mother?"

"Nothing, Mama," he said. But this was not genuine, because at this age there were ten thousand things he'd rather do than chauffeur his scowling, chastising mother all over Buffalo. Lately he wondered about meeting girls and dating. He had never gone to his senior prom. Loretta said he wasn't ready for it. Told him it was a sin for unmarried folk to be dancing and touching like that—in fact, those heathens were fortunate not to have been struck down in the middle of a step-back slide.

But still, an overpowering lust for female flesh kept bursting through the zippers of Shadrack's pants. To pleasure himself he conjured visions of all sorts of ladies. Young and old. Big and small. Light and dark. It felt strange to him, this desire, this painful want of a woman, because nothing in life had ever occupied his mind so much. Even the ugly ones. The nasty ones. The crack addicts and prostitutes. He wanted them all. Needed them so badly he felt dizzy when he couldn't find some private place, some bathroom stall, to masturbate in. Luckily, it was around this time he met a busty young woman from the east side and took her to bed. Their meeting happened quite by chance.

When the known hustler Mitch Jones was found bloodied and dead on Beech Street in the Fruit Belt, his family members insisted on a quick funeral. No frills. No expense. Some of them being Christian folks, they maintained that a two-bit hustling dope dealer ought not have too much.

"Yeah, we knew this was coming," a group of them said to Harold Niederpruem and Shadrack in the funeral director's office. "We washed our hands of this boy a long time ago. Can't say we all that sad to see him dead. Wrap him up real good in a cardboard box, Mister Undertaker. Use his bones as firewood if you want. Whatever you do, make sure the devil can't send him back."

In the end, some people are eulogized and buried. Some people get dumped in the ground. And because Mitch Jones, the deceased, had failed at one of life's fundamental goals, namely to outlive everyone who could possibly embarrass him at his funeral, he almost suffered the latter. But despite what the relatives had asked for, Harold Niederpruem provided a nice pine casket, two purple wreaths, several sprays of yellow and white carnations, and enshrouded the young man in a three-piece suit, even though a relative had only sent over a pair of denim jeans and a basketball jersey. The organ wept a quiet rendition of *It is Well with My Soul*. In Chapel B, after a brief dedication and eulogy, the family gathered round the casket and bade farewell. Shadrack set a few carnations inside and sealed the young man in for all eternity.

Such funerals were common at The Blessed Home, and this one wouldn't have been of much consequence either had Shadrack not come to know Syreeta Jones, the half-sister of the deceased—a shapely woman of medium height, dark-skinned, with a big, broad thicket of permed hair and an exposed midriff. Her lips were full and glossy, and she didn't so much walk as glide, swaying, buttocks dipping and rolling, catching everyone's attention, even the jealous gazes of the women. For much of the funeral, Shadrack had been watching her—that curvature of her hips, the rise and thickness of her backside—and it wasn't until she confronted him during the recessional that he realized she must have known all along.

"You clocking me like I stole something," Syreeta said, shifting all her weight to one hip. She wore false eyelashes, and her glittering fingernails were a mix of gold and scarlet. Heavy hoop earrings elongated the lobes of her ears. "Well, can I help you, sir?" she said.

And by twilight, the two of them were at Roosevelt Park, fumbling around in the back seat of the Citation, doing things that heaped delirium over Shadrack's body.

"Do you really like me?" Syreeta said with a beautiful smile, right before he entered. And Shadrack said yes because what she had to give was something he couldn't do without. It was the moment you arrived at the Pearly Gates and the angel asked if you'd lived a good life, and you said yes because what else would you say? The simple lie offered too much reward, and was far more apropos than any stammering explanation of the truth.

But the quick ejaculation caused him pain.

"You okay, handsome?" Syreeta said.

"A little lightheaded."

"Breathe." She massaged his shoulders and neck. "Relax."

Shadrack couldn't decide whether the soreness in his groin felt good or bad, or whether he should be proud or ashamed of what he and Syreeta had done. "I thought girls didn't like doing that," he said.

"It's all right if we say it's all right."

Shadrack noticed the scent of her. He hadn't perceived it during those frantic moments, but it was there now, pungent and stalled, and he wondered whether it was normal or whether Syreeta had a problem of some sort. The instant clarity and calm—the bizarre feeling that all of the urgency had gone out of the world—this surprised him. And for some reason now, Syreeta's worn-away lipstick and exposed breasts made her seem to him, suddenly, commonplace. The manic lust he had felt only moments before— that raging certainty Syreeta Jones would be his woman forever—it had completely dissipated, and he was content to simply wipe up the mess and get home before long.

"Now you wanna leave?" Syreeta said. She released his neck. "You some kind of player? I thought you was different."

"Different from what?"

"Every other dude who wanna leave. Same old story."

Shadrack couldn't figure out what he'd done wrong. He would have thought she was ready to go, too. Their business was done there, and Roosevelt Park wasn't the safest place to be at that hour. "Isn't your mother wondering where you are?" he said. He thought of his own mother.

"You know what hurts me, Shadrack?" Syreeta said. "Guys who leave. Deep down they all want a woman like me. Yeah, I might not be all sweet and proper, but I know how to make a guy happy, how to feel good. Problem is, after they happy and feel good, they always wanna leave. That hurts."

"What do you want me to do?"

"Stay with me a little while," she said. "Talk to me some. Can you do that?"

When Shadrack didn't move, Syreeta caressed his shoulders again and told him everything about herself. How over the years, she had become accustomed to funerals. Since the early eighties alone, four members of her family had been murdered. Two others committed suicide. The rest, many of whom believed in the utility of guns and knives when settling disputes, would probably meet their fates in similar fashion.

She and her deceased half-brother shared the same father, a big time mack daddy named Orphus Jones, who would probably be serving a life sentence for murder if he weren't already dead himself.

"They say he fathered twelve children with nine different women," Syreeta said. "But he only married once, far as I know. That was to my mama. Her name is Zora."

Zora Jones, she explained, breathed more cigarette smoke than clean air, and sometimes sold her government food stamps for cash when she had no money for a pack of Virginia Slims. The two of them lived on the east side in the Kenfield Projects, a neighborhood apparently on the verge of being conquered by rodents.

"Boy, we got more rats over there than people," Syreeta said laughing. "My mama be hollering at them rats. Cussing like a drunk stepdaddy. Laying down poison and everything. But guess what? Them big ol' rats eat that poison like candy and keep going." She laughed again. "So then she put down traps. One night we heard one of them snap, and when we went to look, my mama's house slipper was in it. Can you believe that? Damn critters put my mama's house slipper in the trap! That, my friend, is what you call a rat problem."

Syreeta was not ashamed of where she grew up. After all, her best friends were from Kenfield and so were her best memories. Besides, many good people lived in those projects, and some of them spent their entire lives there and never had a complaint. But she herself, now, had come to desire something different for her life. A real house. A real family. And as the relationship progressed over the next several weeks, she made it abundantly clear.

"I don't feel good, Shadrack," Syreeta said. They were at Roosevelt Park again, but this time she locked her knees and straightened out the hem of her skirt. "I might be pregnant."

"Already?"

"Only takes once, homeboy," she said. "I wanna get married."

"We just met—"

Syreeta flipped up a palm. "Don't go there. If I'm good enough to screw, I'm good enough to marry."

"But you haven't even met my mother."

"On the serious tip, Shadrack. What's up with all this sex we been having, what does it mean? I don't do this with everybody. Am I your woman, or are we just . . . " she threw up her fingers like quotes, "kicking it?"

"I don't know, Syreeta. I just thought—"

"Thought what, that you was just having a good time?"

"I don't know. Maybe we'll get married. But not so soon, right?"

"Like I said, I don't do this with everybody. You need to tell me what's up. And yes, I wanna meet your mother right away."

When the name Syreeta Jones was first uttered at home, Loretta popped Shadrack's forehead with a mixing spoon. And when he divulged that his new girlfriend might be pregnant, Loretta spat in his face. "How dare you bring this shame on me?" she said. She stood before him with arms akimbo, the mixing spoon dripping pancake mix onto the floor. After a long reproachful stare, she relented and turned away. "Well, at least I know you not a sissy," she said. "How come you didn't tell me about this girl?"

"Didn't know how you'd react. She wants to get married."

"That's ridiculous. I don't even know this girl. How long you been going with her?"

"About a month now."

"And she pregnant already? Ain't nobody getting married around here. I'm not even married yet. I mean it, Shadrack. No marriage. You can tell her I said it."

On a warm Saturday afternoon Shadrack brought Syreeta home to Loretta, who was sitting on the front porch under the shade of Mattie Turnbull's sugar maple, fanning herself with her sun hat. Her azaleas were in bloom, and a hand-push lawn mower stood in the center of the yard where she must have left it upon noticing them pulling up.

"That's your mama?" Syreeta said. "She looks young."

"She is," Shadrack said.

Some of the neighbors had taken to their porches as well, looking on, and across the street, a single mother and her live-in boyfriend were grilling up some good-smelling sausage in the side yard and playing loud music. Syreeta didn't ask about the crooked railing as she mounted the porch stairs of 99 Peach Street, which was fine with Shadrack since he wouldn't have to hear Loretta tell the same story of how he once slept through the noise of a car crash.

"Pleased to meet you, Miss Ford." Syreeta embraced Loretta and kissed her cheek. "Shadrack talks about you all the time."

"I'm sure." Loretta scrutinized her. Up and down. Studied her belly and then her face again. "She's cute," she said and offered her a seat on a lawn chair next to her.

Shadrack sighed with relief. "I know, Mama. See what I was telling you?"

"Yeah, but cute don't cut it," Loretta said staring straight at Syreeta. "'Cause pretty don't mean a thing if the heart ain't right. What church you go to, sweetheart?"

Shadrack interjected. "She's coming to church with us tomorrow, Mama."

"I reckon Syreeta can speak for herself, Shadrack."

"My family don't go to church like that," Syreeta said. "We just good people. Kind of live a good life, you know?"

"A good life," Loretta said, not in a mocking way but as though she was pondering the meaning of the words. "So tell me, Syreeta. How is it you know my son for only a month and you pregnant already?"

"Well, Miss Ford," Syreeta said, giggling, "all of us know the answer to that one."

"You proud of that?"

"No, I'm not proud. But I'm having Shadrack's baby. I feel he should do right by me."

"Folks marry for a lot of reasons," Loretta said. "Ain't always the right thing to do. Everybody wants to use holy matrimony to clean up a dirty courtship. But when you marry, it's supposed to be because God brought you together. Not to cover up your sin. Now, being that my son been in church all his life and you don't even go to church, I don't see how God could have brought y'all together. Forgive me—and I don't mean to sound close-minded—but I can't condone my son marrying a worldly woman. He knows that."

"With all due respect, Miss Ford. I wouldn't call myself worldly. I might not be in the church and all, but that don't make me a bad woman."

"I didn't say you was a bad woman. I said you can't marry my son. Now if you don't mind I'd like to get back to my garden work."

After months of headaches, nausea, and diarrhea that kept her sprinting to the bathroom and collapsing onto the toilet, Syreeta delivered a precious baby girl named Asia, who resembled Shadrack so much Syreeta said she felt slighted. After eight months of pure misery and fourteen hours of rip-roaring torture, the little chocolate baby had the nerve to come out looking just like the father. Shadrack, being instantly smitten, bought a brand new crib and bassinet, an entire drawer of baby clothes, and a month's worth of formula milk and diapers, and then took Syreeta everywhere she needed to go and relinquished part of his pay every other week for support.

"Stop leading that girl on," Loretta said, insisting that Shadrack was doing too much. "You making her think she hit the jackpot. She gone think you in love with her."

"It's all for Asia, Mama."

"It's all for show. Now stop it."

Sudden fatherhood was daunting. Moreover, Shadrack felt complicit in the birth of Syreeta's depression, and fully responsible for the well-being of both her and their pitiful, wailing baby girl. This even led him to consider marriage despite what Loretta said. But the fact remained that while he had already embarrassed the church by christening a misbegotten child, it would be an even greater sin to marry an unsaved woman. And since Syreeta had little interest in churchgoing, except for maybe once every other month or so, time was not right for a public marriage.

"A worldly heathen," Loretta said. "Act like she just as much woman as me. No marriage, Shadrack. Not that girl. I don't care how many babies she have. Make her get on the altar and get saved."

Ironically, Syreeta's presence at church (once she agreed to come, and even then it was obviously to appease Shadrack) became part of the undoing of their relationship. For it was here she came to meet Deacon Duke Baines, a generous bachelor in his late sixties. And before long, rumors abounded that Syreeta wasn't staying home and that she had been seen sneaking out of the old man's house on several occasions. Sister Mayhew, the Sunday school teacher, saw it first. Then Sister Daisy, the head usher. And then Brother Thompson, who lived right next door to the man. All of them had the same story everybody else had: Deacon Duke Baines, a fellow known to pay for the company of young ladies, was buying time from Syreeta Jones. When Shadrack confronted her, Syreeta dismissed it all as nonsense and asked why any girl would want a broken-down, smelly old man such as Deacon Duke Baines.

But apparently many of them did.

Having never had a wife or children, Deacon Duke Baines had worked many years at General Motors and earned enough pension to live out a cheerful retirement in the company of barely-legal women. He lived in a large house on Michigan Avenue and owned several houses over in the Fruit Belt, which he leased to various members of the church. He bought his Buicks with cash in hand, and visitors to his home swore up and down they spotted giant pickle barrels full of money in his pantry.

He was not a very spiritual man though, and though he served as chairman of the Trustee Board and vice-president of the Gethsemane Male Chorus, he was more likely to be found passed out on the bar at Foster's Lounge than bowed down before the altar during Friday night prayer. All the same, he was a pillar of the church, a long-time member, who inherited his chairmanship from his father who had been the head deacon for many years before passing away. His mother, also well regarded, had directed the senior choir for decades until she literally slumped forward and died at the church piano one Sunday. Moreover, it was well known that Deacon Duke Baines gave more money in tithes and offerings than anyone else at Gethsemane could possibly afford to give. As a result, the church bookstore was named in his honor, his mother's name was engraved on the piano bench where she once sat, a picture of his father hung in the foyer next to Reverend Shropshire's picture, and each time he pulled his gleaming brown Buick into the church lot, he parked in a spot labeled RESERVED FOR CHAIRMAN BAINES.

For the most part, folks at Gethsemane frowned on his whoremongering. Even considered him too self-absorbed to be a head deacon. Nevertheless, they had reached a unanimous verdict: that despite his faults and vanity, all of his whoremongering and drinking, he was, at heart, a genuinely kind man. He helped people. When they fell on hard times, they could count on him to lend money. He treated kids well. Remembered their birthdays. Gave them candy. All good report cards earned five dollars. Even his tenants, most of whom were single mothers and elderly widows, discovered that rent day fell on whichever day they happened to have enough money to pay it. All of this goodness, the saints agreed, typified Deacon Duke Baines. So whenever a new rumor emerged about him seducing some young woman at the church, the folks at Gethsemane handled it delicately. They didn't ignore the charge, but a reasonable explanation would usually suffice.

"Listen here, Reverend," Deacon Duke Baines said during an open meeting in the pastor's office. Some of the saints desired clarification on the issue of Syreeta Jones. "My family built this church. I'll be damned if anybody gone put me out of it. Y'all hear me?" He crossed his feet on Reverend Shropshire's desk. "Now, I never touched that girl. What is she, nineteen? Twenty? I'd be plain sick going after a girl that young. Ain't none of it true at all, Reverend. None of it."

But it had to be true. Otherwise, no one would have seen Syreeta sneaking out of his house. Confronted by this common sense logic, but also the equally plausible conclusion that Deacon Duke Baines and Syreeta barely knew each other and couldn't possibly have become lovers, Shadrack didn't know what to believe. When he went to his mother crestfallen over these suspicions, Loretta told him he was stupid for trusting what people say.

"Your ego is bruised is all," she said nonchalantly. She was reading scripture and drinking tea. "If you didn't see it, don't accuse."

"Would she do something like that, Mama? Would she take Asia over there?"

"Maybe," Loretta said. "Maybe not. That's the problem with a worldly woman. Laid with you so easy, now you can't trust her. Should have listened to me."

"If it's true, I want custody of Asia. I can raise her myself."

"Shadrack, you don't know the first thing about raising kids, let alone a girl." Loretta looked up from her Bible. "Besides, I won't let you take a woman's baby from her, even if it *is* true. Forget about that."

Sunday night, after the Buffalo Bills lost the Super Bowl for the fourth straight year, this time by seventeen points to the Dallas Cowboys, the streets of the city were as quiet as the chapels of The Blessed Home. Snowflakes were falling. Shadrack scraped frost from the car windows and wing mirrors, and used a pitcher of warm water to unfreeze the lock on the door. The engine took a long time to start up. When it finally sparked and stayed running, Shadrack drove off into the slick, mournful avenues that led to Syreeta's place in Kenfield.

"Did you take Asia over there?" he said at the door.

Syreeta gave him her back. "Don't bother me." She rocked Asia on her shoulder and eased herself back to a seat in front of the television. It was tuned to the post-game show. Having no more stomach for the Buffalo Bills and their fourth consecutive Super Bowl defeat, Shadrack flicked through a bunch of channels and settled on an episode of *The Simpsons*.

"I was watching it," Syreeta said.

"You don't even like football."

Asia was sleeping, swaddled in a pink baby blanket and smelling of talcum powder. When Shadrack reached for her, Syreeta leaned away. "What you come here for, Shadrack?"

"Can't I hold my daughter?"

"She's asleep."

"I want to know if you took her over there."

Syreeta preferred to discuss the next child support check. The current biweekly amount wasn't enough. The Pampers and formula were running out, and she hadn't applied for WIC or welfare yet.

"I don't make a whole lot, Syreeta."

"Cost of Pampers don't go down just 'cause Shadrack don't make a lot."

"Can you breastfeed and save me some money?"

"I don't want my titties getting saggy like my mother's."

"But that's what they're made for, Syreeta. To feed a baby, not to be cute with."

"Okay, well, keep your hands off of them then."

"Did you take Asia to that man's house?"

"You don't respect me, do you?" Syreeta said. "Like I'm so desperate I'd screw a man old enough to be my granddaddy. Like some cheap whore. And then take my baby with me? You must be tripping. How you gone come here and diss me like that?" She smacked her teeth. "Anyways, homeboy, if you took care of business, instead of busting your nuts after seven seconds, you wouldn't be worried about me fucking somebody else. There, that's your answer."

"You didn't have to go there, Syreeta."

"I went there. So step off. We ain't married. So don't ask where I been."

"I have a right to know about my daughter."

"You don't got a right to know shit, Shadrack. All you got a right to know is my mailing address to send me those checks. 'Cause from now on, sucker, if you wanna spend time with *my* baby, you need to come correct with *my* money. That is, unless, or until, you got a big fat diamond-studded ass ring to put on *my* finger. Otherwise, step." The commotion started to wake Asia. Syreeta lowered the television volume, and then stroked Asia's curly hair and rocked her back to sleep. "Anything else you wanna know?"

"I want to keep Asia with me for a little while."

Syreeta scoffed at him. "Nigger, you insane. Touch my baby and I'll have you locked up before you reach that door."

After two weeks of not seeing Syreeta and Asia, Shadrack grew despondent. Syreeta ignored his calls. He left messages, but Syreeta never called back. The only sign of life he received was an official letter from Family Court demanding his appearance at a child support hearing. When he couldn't reach Syreeta for an explanation, he showed up unannounced and invited her out for the evening so they could talk about moving in together.

They agreed to leave the baby at home with Syreeta's mother, Zora Jones, who pulled her cigarette from her mouth and blew smoke toward Shadrack's face. "Never fails," Zora Jones said. "Make a nigger pay some child support, all of sudden he wanna talk things over."

It was late February. Snow-draped tree limbs stretched out over the avenues. Shadrack and Syreeta drove to Skate Land Roller Rink on East Ferry Street near Main. It was Hip Hop Throwback Night, and the music was audible all the way down the block. More than two hundred teenagers had packed into the hall, swaying under the strobe lights. At the turntables, a DJ was scratching records while an overweight rapper blustered into a microphone about the girls on his jock. He was *cold chillin'*, he said, *rockin' the mic*, and would beat down all the perpetrators and sucker MCs if they wanted to battle him. And then he cupped a hand to his mouth and beatboxed in front of a whooping horde of teenagers.

After snacking on some pepperoni slices and soda, Shadrack asked Syreeta whether she wanted to skate, but the line for skate rentals was long, and she preferred to join the crowd near the turntables.

"You know I can't dance," Shadrack said.

"Fine. Catch up later then." When a clearing opened, Syreeta shimmied onto the dance floor. Her pulsing, buxom figure became the center of attention.

"Work that booty, girl," someone blurted out. "Shake it like it's your birthday."

One dancer stepped forward and bounced his groin against her backside. A masculine celebration erupted around them. Syreeta whirled around to the dancer. When Shadrack saw her smiling at the young man, and swirling her hips the same way she always did during sex, and making the same expressions she always made when it felt good, he charged forward, jostling through the crowd, and seized her arm.

"Get off me," Syreeta yelled. "You ain't my husband." She yanked her arm away and danced even wilder.

Shadrack took hold of her with both hands. "Stop disrespecting me," he said. "You're acting like a whore. What is wrong with you?"

"I said get off me." Syreeta wrenched away again. Doing so, she lost her balance and stumbled to the floor, something that must have seemed to everyone else like a shove. The young male dancer dipped away from the tussle. People in the crowd jeered at Shadrack.

A security guard appeared at the scene. "Man, you crazy? You better check yourself. She can have you arrested, fool."

"Don't ever call me again," Syreeta hollered from the floor. "You don't have a daughter anymore. You hear me, dammit!" And with a storm of words, she battered the ramparts of his manhood. Seized upon his most shameful inadequacies only to make them known to this heckling crowd. But even though this brand of humiliation could have unmanned the most self-assured of men, Shadrack barely processed the rebukes. For a strange remembrance had come over him, that of the silence of a twelve-year-old boy prisoned upstairs. At once, he felt ashamed; then contrite; and then, oddly, comforted and redeemed. For though he hadn't actually pushed Loretta (well, Syreeta) he felt good about her fall. Felt good about turning the tables a bit. At last, he had stood up for that little boy upstairs and told that abusive woman (whatever her name was) to stop hurting him.

9

Syreeta Jones didn't much like popping her fingers and swinging her behind around in public. It grew tiresome after a while. But future sexual partners were so aroused by it she saw no reason not to do it. A future sexual partner was what others called a man. But she had long given up on finding one of those (a real man, that is) and referred to each as what he really was: a future sexual partner, or not. No one could blame her for this attitude toward men, and toward relationships in general, because at fourteen the Hollywood Star on the Streets had taught her there was no such thing as love and that the power that resided between her thick, dark legs was about the only thing of worth she'd ever come to possess. He never said this directly. It would have been too callous a thing for a father to say. But his business was knowing such things. And Syreeta, studying him over the years, could only conclude that being loved by a man was impossible, especially when she didn't know if her father did.

For much of Syreeta's early life, the Hollywood Star on the Streets remained a mystery to her. People would ask, "Where is your daddy?"

And she would respond, "Nowhere."

"Say what?"

"I said nowhere." This meant either he was nowhere to be found or didn't want to be found, neither explanation being unusual for a man with twelve children by nine different women. When she had the rare opportunity to ask why he spent so little time with her and so much time in the streets, he made no apologies. "Pimping and hustling is in my blood, baby girl," he would say. "Only thing I can do about it is do it."

In Syreeta's earliest recollections of him, his fingernails were too long for a man, and his hands were made of gold, or shining with gold jewelry, she would later realize. Each time he bent down, she would run her fingers through his long crimpy hair and stroke the fur of his full-length mink coat. He was a man who paid no attention to the price of things and seemed to wipe money from his hands like dirt. And though never known to hold a job, he somehow had the means to drive a brand new Cadillac and pay cash for a suite he resided in at the Hyatt.

In those days when Kenfield folk said he was a bad man, they meant it. But not it the way people outside Kenfield would have thought. For though it was rumored he once sliced a man's throat and left him to die on the shoulder of the Kensington Expressway, people in Kenfield didn't see him as a criminal. To them, the loud suits, the souped-up cars, and the sexy fair-skinned women all made him more of a Hollywood star on the streets, and so they took to calling him that. One man might plead to another, "Come on, man. You know who I'm talking about. Orphus Jones. The Hollywood Star on the Streets." And he would walk sly like him and say "baby" and "partner" like him, and then the other man would know exactly who it was.

"Oh yeah, Hollywood," he would answer in a hip falsetto. "That's a bad man you talking about there. Big time player, baby. Bad to the *bone*."

No one knew how many women were obsessed with him, though most people still contended that he had only married once. That was to Syreeta's mother, Zora, who, more than anything else, hated the man's other children. At least eleven others were out there, and she despised them all. It wasn't that Zora Jones was a cruel woman. She took no pleasure in hating innocent children (even if they were bastard children), but children came equipped with mothers, all of whom competed for Hollywood's attention. And being that most of those mothers were hookers and drug addicts who would never be married to him like she was, she, Zora Jones, was better than all of them, which naturally meant her child, Syreeta, was better, too—not that anyone could convince Hollywood of that. For most times, he ignored all of his children equally. Other times, he favored Mitch, his eldest child and closest son, whom he taught along with Syreeta not to believe in love.

One night when Mitch was drowning in misery over a cheating girlfriend, the Hollywood Star on the Streets drove him and Syreeta to the corner of Elmwood and Chippewa and found Spring, a baby-faced hooker so smitten with Hollywood he barely had to speak the request. Nevertheless, he did, and she obliged.

"You don't have to watch if you don't want," Hollywood said to Syreeta. But she never looked away from the foggy glass. The car rocked in a steady rhythm. Spring's skinny bare legs were wrapped high around Mitch's back, bobbing with the rhythm of the car. Afterward, Hollywood sent Spring away with a kiss and handed Mitch a reefer to smoke. Mitch slouched in the back seat, sweating, his face clear as an answered question.

"Use one woman," Hollywood said to him, "to get the other one off your mind. When you find yourself in love, you'd best put a bullet in that bitch's head and move on. Or else you gone put one in your own head someday." Hollywood reached over and retrieved the reefer. "In this business, your game gotta be tight. Your shit gotta be cold as ice. Ain't no time for love."

"You can't never tell a girl you love her?" Mitch said, his visage still fresh with the afterglow of his encounter with Spring.

"Tell her whatever she need to hear, partner. Just don't love her."

When Syreeta met Mitch's best friend, Hot Sauce, a future sexual partner, and started seeing him, the Hollywood Star on the

Streets took her for another ride. Only the two of them this time.

"Naw, baby girl," he said. "Can't happen. Not Hot Sauce. He a street nigger. Girl like you need somebody square."

"Hot Sauce is different from the rest of the guys. He said he love me."

"What I tell you about that?" Hollywood steered to the side of the road and threw the gearstick into park. "Look, if you had a million dollars, would you trust him to hold it overnight?"

"I wouldn't trust nobody with a million dollars."

"So how you gone trust him with your future? Forget Hot Sauce. Forget about love. Get somebody square."

"What if I fall in love with the square dude?"

"You won't," he said. "He'll never treat you bad enough."

They cruised the east side that night, collecting from all his women out on the track. "Break yourself, baby," he would say, and each would surrender from her bosom a crumpled, sweaty stash of assorted bills. They were delighted to do it. Proud to see their hard-earned cash fold into the pocket of the number one mack daddy in town. Sometimes a disaffected hooker from another stable tried to pass him money when her pimp wasn't around, but Hollywood declined, and told her to take that measly scratch home to her people.

"I don't need every hoe that's out on the stroll," he explained to Syreeta when she asked why he would pass up the money. "A hoe that hop from pimp to pimp can't be trusted. Same with Hot Sauce. You can't trust him. Can't trust nobody in this world. Never forget that, even when you square up. Gain people's trust, but don't return the favor. Never believe what anybody tell you. Only believe what you already know. You don't come to the streets to make friends, baby girl. You come out here to keep your enemies in check."

Everywhere they went, people venerated Hollywood and spoke with the same deference with which they addressed preachers and school principals. Wherever he parked, neighborhood boys ran to open his car door and beamed when he slipped them a dollar bill or two. Folks stepped aside so he could pass, and when he did, they couldn't stop staring at his sly, loose-limbed walk, his mink coat, the matching fur hat. Even the passed-out junkies on the corner had the presence of mind to sit up when his freshly polished alligators coasted by. Because Orphus Jones was a bad man. Like some kind of Hollywood star on the streets. And nobody had the nerve to say he wasn't.

All of this made Syreeta feel powerful. If her father was somebody, then she was somebody too. Although she didn't have him with her all the time, or even half the time, she at least carried his name and reputation wherever she went, and in a neighborhood that was all but collectively fatherless in those days, a girl with a prominent father was queen among all peers. But it turned out Hollywood relished the attention far less than Syreeta did.

"Ain't no happy endings in these streets," he told her. "Stay away from your brother's friends. They're nothing but bad news." He pulled on a joint until his eyeballs were glazed and distant. "To be honest, I'm not gone do this much longer myself. About time to lay low. Niggers wanna kill me. White man trying to put me in jail. Kind of get tired after a while. One day I'm gone hitch a ride to other side of the world and never come back."

Syreeta had never heard him so wistful. "You gone leave me?" she said. "Can I come too? Where you going?"

"Not sure. Maybe Africa. Spain. Asia. I don't know yet, but I'm going."

"Ain't no niggers and white folks in Asia," Syreeta said.

Hollywood tittered. "Yeah, that's where I'm headed, baby girl. Asia. Far away from here. Don't tell nobody where I'm at."

But he never made it out of Buffalo. In fact, he never made it out of Zora Jones's bedroom one night, all because he had moved a new woman into his suite at the Hyatt—a woman half her age—which was a great offense. Because what the Hollywood Star on the Streets had apparently forgotten was that the only thing that ever infuriated a woman was the thought of a much younger one, and that to have another woman is not necessarily fatal, but to treat another woman better most certainly is. So when he lay lifeless on Zora Jones's bed, the half-finished glass of bourbon still on the nightstand, the woman showed no remorse, and as Syreeta tried to shake life back into her father's body, her mother stood by with no urgency in her voice at all.

"Best thing for him, really," Zora Jones said, staring down at him. "He wasn't happy no way."

Syreeta sprinted out into the dark, snow-filled streets with no shoes and no inclination to disclose anything. For though there rose up within her a crimson hatred for her mother, she could not afford to lose two parents in the same night. So she never voiced her suspicions, and no one ever checked her father's blood for rat poison, because if The Hollywood Star on the Streets had been murdered, the police figured it was long overdue.

In the years that followed, Syreeta made her money from the older men in the neighborhood. Unlike young dudes, older men were willing to pay for it—pay a whole lot for it—and couldn't care less who got it afterward. She used foam to stave off pregnancy. Other girls wanted to be locked down waiting on monthly welfare checks, but she was different. Like Hollywood, she was too good to beg for crumbs when she could be out getting the whole pie. And between Mitch, Hot Sauce, and the money she made fucking all the older men in the neighborhood, she had everything she needed.

Now if Orphus Jones was the original Hollywood Star on the Streets, his son Mitch was more like the stodgy understudy no one had paid to see. A shorter, less handsome substitute. If Hollywood was the mack daddy CEO of the ghetto, then Mitch was no more than a mailroom clerk. If the venerated father was once king of the Kenfield Projects, well then Mitch was the son everyone expected would bring down the monarchy. For he and Hot Sauce treated hustling like a parlor game, not the live-or-die criminal enterprise it was. They smoked themselves higher than the highs of the people they sold crack to. Let broke women pay with sex instead of money—something his father warned him not to do. Recruited grade school kids to be lookouts and dealers. Even assassinated the most casual of rivals for no good cause. It was thus no surprise both of them eventually found themselves staring at the wrong end of a glock-nine.

Hot Sauce met his fate the evening he and Syreeta were parked outside a liquor store on Genesee Street smoking a blunt. The setting sun glowed copper all over the horizon. A Range Rover eased up to the driver's side window. Hot Sauce didn't notice. But Syreeta did, and recognized the young man riding in the passenger seat. He went by the name Cool Breeze. A sleazy hustler who'd been jocking her since the day her father died. Handsome enough. Persuasive. But he was a young man, and she already had one of those—at least until Cool Breeze fired through the glass. The shot left Hot Sauce flopped over in Syreeta's lap, hemorrhaging from the bullet wound in his head. The pulsating blood soaked her hands and thighs like spilled wine. Hot Sauce was gone. Syreeta recognized the bareness of a face that had no soul—something she observed without screaming because she hadn't yet taken a breath. Cool Breeze swung around to the passenger door and pulled it open.

"Come on, girl," he said, offering his hand. When she didn't move, he said it again. "Come on. He didn't deserve you."

Stunned, but relieved to be alive, Syreeta supposed she had no choice but to extend the blood-soaked hand he so eagerly wanted. The courtship lasted the length of the drive to an apartment on Hempstead Avenue in Kenfield. Syreeta remained voiceless even as Cool Breeze and his partner took turns. Everything had happened so quickly—the murder, the drive, the sex. Later, as she showered, she heard the bathroom door open. Cool Breeze drew back the shower curtain and offered her a towel. "That sucker fucked one of my girls," he said. His eyes moved across her nakedness.

"I woulda gave you what you wanted," Syreeta said. "You didn't have to kill him." Her own voice surprised her. She hadn't uttered a single word since the moment before Hot Sauce was shot.

"Somebody diss you in the hood, you gotta kill him," he said. "But I got you, Syreeta. Stay with me. You gone be my bottom hoe. The main one. Don't worry about nothing. You with Cool Breeze now."

Syreeta stayed with him three days and three nights, until the shock wore off and the smell of his reefer reminded her of her father and brother.

"Here's what I want you to do . . ." Mitch told her when she snuck and called him. And she did exactly what he said. She waited until Cool Breeze got drunk and fell asleep, and then propped open the front door for Mitch and his crew. They crept in, drew their guns, and executed Cool Breeze with eighteen shots to his body. One shot was enough to kill him. The other seventeen would keep the casket closed. But it didn't end there. Associates of Cool Breeze now came after Mitch. They set him up in the usual manner. Sent some shapely beauty his way, then ambushed him. By the time Mitch realized the trickery, he was bleeding out on the pavement outside his home.

His death frightened Syreeta, and as she sat in Chapel B of The Blessed Home, only halfway hearing the eulogy, she wondered where her life was going. She had grown sick of these funeral parlors, these dead faces, the sad dirges of those weeping organs. Was this all life amounted to, premature death? Was this all *she* would amount to, being some sleazy hustler's bottom hoe? She needed a change. Something radically different. And it had to happen quickly.

This was the reason she confronted the young funeral parlor worker who hadn't stopped gawking at her since she walked in. He bore the appearance of the marrying type, which was what she needed. A square dude she couldn't fall in love with. He wasn't handsome and strapping the way she wanted a future sexual partner to be. But when it came to working men, you had to take them in whatever form they came, which sometimes meant a tad too small and not so cute.

This shy young man—an experiment of sorts—was her way out of these funerals. The aversion of whatever misfortune lay waiting in the corridors of her Destiny. She didn't want to be on welfare like her mother, depending on the government and relying on some pimp to do right by her. There had to be another way. And that way was marriage. A real marriage, where the husband woke up early every day and went to work. A man she could be proud of even when they ventured outside the neighborhood. Sure, she had been with some of the finest, most impressive young hustlers in Kenfield, but they were useless outside the ghetto. Against the backdrop of mainstream society, they were strikingly out of place, walking funny now, swaggering like clowns when they passed by proper men. Their words no longer sounded fluid and persuasive, and society didn't give a damn who they were or what they wanted. In other words, Syreeta longed for something other than a future sexual partner. Something more than grown men named Hot Sauce and Cool Breeze. And the square, innocent funeral parlor worker in the back was that other, that more. Of course, she would have to put on some. Burnish the rough edges a bit. Otherwise, he would think she wasn't good enough to take as a wife.

Getting the young man to relieve himself in the back seat of his car was easy. Convincing him to marry her, she found out, was much harder. Arousing his penis required almost no work at all. Getting him to the Justice of the Peace was damn near impossible, especially with his Holy Roller asshole-of-a-mother getting in the way. Even after the birth of Asia, Shadrack still wouldn't marry, which made Syreeta wonder why she ever bothered trying to be something she wasn't. Moreover, she came to dislike her daughter. Asia gave her headaches, wailing like a fire engine all night long. Wouldn't shut up for days sometimes, constantly spitting out her pacifier to scream for more milk, more diapers, more cuddling, or even nothing at all.

One night, Syreeta, while shedding her own tears, thought about throwing Asia away. A garbage dumpster perhaps, or Lake Erie. Deep in the soil of some abandoned lot. Anywhere those wide-mouth, tongue-flailing screams couldn't find her ears. One moment of peace to retain her sanity was all Syreeta asked for, pleaded for. A little rest to recover from this endless insomnia. But Asia didn't understand, and trying to explain these things to a baby was a miserable waste of time. So Syreeta simply decided not to cooperate with Shadrack. Why should she? He knew her troubles but didn't care. If he did, he would help her, marry her, and stop acting as if he were too good.

Had things been different, and had she truly been fond of Shadrack to begin with, Syreeta wouldn't have done what she did with that old man. Had she not been bitter about Shadrack's stubbornness, she would have paid no attention when Deacon Duke Baines approached her at church claiming he had a gift for her and the baby. "Got something real nice for you," he had whispered when no one was around. "Don't tell your boyfriend, though. He might get jealous."

The gift turned out to be thirty dollars for a quiet hand job in the back entranceway of his house. So later, when Syreeta swore she'd never slept with Deacon Duke Baines, she was technically telling the truth. For the old man never tore at her panties the way most men did. He merely reached for her hands and fastened them to his erection. Each time he summoned her, she raised the price, and he paid it without a fuss. Actually, Syreeta could have survived without the money, but she did it anyway. It was a reason to be away from Asia. A way to trade the screams of an infant who needed constant attention for the gentle moans of an old man who didn't want to be heard. This she needed more than money.

Now with so much dysfunction going on, it was hard to pinpoint when things finally spun out of control. Before long, she had become the same old Syreeta Jones again, running the streets, tricking for money. Moreover, the need to escape the depression landed her into the welcoming arms of a crack addiction. For days and weeks at a time, she smoked away life in a crack house near Martin Luther King Park. Years passed, and this was about all she did. It was basic survival. The Hollywood Star on the Streets had taught her everything she needed to know. Don't wait for happy endings, have a heart that's cold as ice, and put a bullet in somebody's head when you fall in love.

10

Bernadine cast her gaze across the table at Giselle, who hadn't touched her Kung Pao chicken. They were dining among the lunch crowd at Ming Dynasty, though Bernadine didn't need to read a fortune cookie to know that Giselle's lack of appetite these days had something, if not everything, to do with Charles Vargas. She had grown thin with grief and hadn't bothered with makeup. For weeks, no one had seen her outside of work. She hadn't answered her door and hadn't called anyone. Even missed Sunday dinner for the first time since she and Eric moved out on their own. Such anomalies would have been the wicked handiwork of only one man.

"If you tell me, I can help," Bernadine said.

The waitress passed by, asking whether everything was all right with the food.

Giselle sighed and nodded. Her eyes had the wear of many sleepless nights. "I went to see him," she said. "A while ago."

"So he's back in town."

"For now I suppose."

"That explains the crappy weather."

"Mother . . . "

"I mean it explains why you've been so glum."

"It was innocent," Giselle said. "Eric had asked about him. I just wanted him to make some time for his son. That's the only reason I went."

"It's understandable, love. Any mother would do the same. Go on."

Bernadine listened. Giselle's voice sounded sad, but she had much to say, rolling out the story like the text of an ancient scroll. How one of Audwin's girlfriends had spotted Charles Vargas out one night, and knew where Giselle could find him. Every Saturday evening he and his band played a gig at Club Mélange on Kensington Avenue, an upbeat soul lounge in the heart of the east side. No one expected to find him there, because the manager was known to pay band members only fifty dollars a night, while Harlem Club on Utica would have paid eighty-five. But they only paid with check, and such an arrangement would have been anathema to a man like Charles Vargas. Having six children, two ex-wives (soon to be three), and child support arrears totaling in the thousands, he could never afford the paper trail of legitimate pay. The county would take it before he saw a dime. So he was forced to settle for less to have more.

"Rather pathetic way to make a living," Bernadine said.

"That's what they do now. Work under the table to avoid child support."

"Can't you report him?"

"For fifty dollars? It's not worth it."

"It's the principle, love."

"He'd just quit and go work somewhere else."

"I see," Bernadine said. "Continue, my dear."

It was the night of the annual bachelor bid. Women of all ages had packed the lounge to its walls, chattering, dancing, calling out to the waiters for more drinks. Giselle had settled toward the back at a table of women she didn't know, but they served as good camouflage while she kept an eye on Charles Vargas and his band.

Nine bachelors swaggered into the hall, greeted by a boisterous applause. The sudden swell of R&B sent more women scooting onto the dance floor. One of them, dressed in tight leather pants and a low cut blouse, was showing off her curves to Charles Vargas, swaying so close he could probably smell the bare skin beneath her perfume.

"Got a little jealous, dear?" Bernadine said.

"Not at all, Mother. I was there for Eric."

The auctioneer, a short round woman in glittering-red, clomped up to the podium in her high heels. "Listen here, ladies," she said in a southern drawl. "We know money can't buy love. But tonight, money can and *will* buy you a date with one of these fine men."

"You sure they all single?" someone shouted.

"They sure is, girlfriend," the auctioneer said. "We did background checks on all of them. Fingerprints. Blood tests. Urine tests. Everything." The women in the crowd found this hilarious.

As the band played, the auctioneer introduced the first bachelor, a handsome, brown-skinned man in his mid-twenties, who kicked his way forward and did the Running Man in front of a sea of waving dollar bills. The back and forth stopped at three hundred dollars, and the winning lady escorted him to her table. The next bachelor, six-foot-three, stripped off his jacket and struck a pose. Cameras flashed. The bidding started. He went for three hundred and seventy-five. His date seized him by the hand and led him straight out of the main door of Club Mélange.

Excitement warmed the air, and it was hard to hear the auctioneer when she announced the third bachelor—a schoolteacher or something, late-thirties, light-skinned. He burst completely out of his shirt before a throng of screaming women. His chest was not firm, nor was his belly, but the women still cheered, fanning the air with their dollar bills. He sold for two hundred and fifty to a middle-aged woman wearing a wedding ring.

Bachelors kept performing. The auctioneer kept inviting bids. Women in the lounge kept cheering and dancing and strutting away with their dates. And then without warning, in the middle of the screaming and just before the bridge to the next chorus, Giselle felt someone's rugged gaze. Charles Vargas had spotted her from across the crowded lounge. His penetrating brown eyes showed no emotion, and he only nodded as if to say hey, and then turned his attention back to the band.

"Guess he didn't like you crashing the party," Bernadine said.

"That's his problem, not mine. Aren't I allowed to be out on a Saturday night?"

"Of course," Bernadine said. She imagined her daughter in that east side lounge, cold and aloof, looking as out of place as Queen Elizabeth might look standing on the corner of Genesee and Chippewa after midnight. And as for Charles Vargas, there in his clever hiding place, having evaded the ambush of responsibility for so long, how disappointing it must have been to catch the scent of it, and then look up and see it baring its teeth right there.

Giselle explained that they met outside during intermission. The night was warm and pleasant. They shared a perfunctory embrace, then strolled away from the lights and sounds of Club Mélange. Cars whizzed by on Kensington Avenue. And up the block there were many houses with porch lights on, and pale light shone through the windows. The neighborhood was awake, though for Giselle and Charles Vargas, a great void lay between them for the longest time.

"When are you getting a real job?" Giselle said, finally.

Charles Vargas took his time and lit up a Newport, and then blew smoke through his nostrils. "What are you doing here, Giselle?"

"Relax, I'm not taking you to court."

"That's what they all say."

"I'm not everybody else, Charles." Giselle remembered the smell of his cigarettes, the way he breathed smoke out of his nose when he was in a bad mood. Not much had changed about him other than the style of his clothes. The timbre of his voice was the same. His hands, his hair, his handsome face. All the same. Other men had come and gone in her life, but none had replicated the impressions Charles Vargas laid on her senses many years ago, and she wondered if he still saw her the same way. "Wouldn't kill you to help out with your kids," Giselle said. "They're yours."

"If you came for money, I don't have any."

"I've never asked you for money. I'm a lawyer. I have my own."

"Good for you. So why are you here?"

"Eric wants to meet his father."

"I never met mine."

"That's no excuse, Charles. Stop talking like that. How could you say that?"

And momentarily, the gaping hole in their conversation came back. A group of teenage boys had congregated at the corner of Kensington and Grider, not causing trouble, just wasting time, and Giselle could hear pieces of their conversation, something about a new girl in the neighborhood, and who was going to get her number first.

"It's hard out here, Giselle. I just don't have anything to give right now."

"Then spend time with him. Stop running. Give up this nightclub life."

"Not happening."

"You want to have regrets when you're older?"

"I don't have to wait till I'm old for regrets. You never had a problem with my music in high school."

"That was a long time ago, Charles."

"So I'm stuck in the past?"

"I don't know *where* you are most times."

And then for some reason he kissed her on the mouth. Perhaps he was drawn to the shimmering lip-gloss she had worn that night, or the new outfit and hairdo, or the glinting, metallic shine of her fingernails. But most likely, he just wanted to change the subject. Giselle nudged him back with her fingertips, and when he tried again, she walked off. "The past is the past, Charles. Make some time for your son."

Later that night he showed up at her door.

"I told him Eric was asleep," Giselle said. "But he wouldn't leave. Started saying his divorce was almost final and that he still loved me and we could get married."

"You believed him, love?"

"No, I didn't," Giselle said. But before she could tell Charles Vargas that, he had already pulled her close. His breath tasted like peppermint, and as they kissed and swooned, Giselle felt a passion flow from her bosom like never before. Before she knew it, she was holding him so tightly she couldn't tell whose sweat was whose or whose naked body was generating so much warmth. And all she thought to say the entire time they made love was, "Charles, I missed you. I missed you so much."

"Then later he told you he was staying with his wife," Bernadine said. She watched her daughter's countenance fall again, and wished like any mother that she herself could take on the pain and relieve her child.

Giselle nodded.

"And he never did spend time with Eric."

"Right," Giselle said. "But he doesn't even love that woman, Mother."

"Doesn't matter, love," Bernadine said. "Some men were born to make women happy. Charles Vargas is not one of those men." Giselle dried her eyes with a table napkin Bernadine placed in her hand. "Reality smacks hard, my dear. I don't mean to sound harsh. But you have to decide what you want. Do you want happiness, or do you want Charles? Do you want fulfillment in life, or do you want Charles? Do you want a husband and a family, or do you want Charles Vargas? That is what you have to decide."

"I'm pregnant again, Mother."

"Lord Almighty." Bernadine felt breathless.

"I'm not keeping it."

When Bernadine collected enough breath to ask why, Giselle said she had no choice. In one lifetime, she couldn't make the same awful mistake twice. The unborn had to go. Single motherhood had already cost too much. More than anything, she wanted a husband. But most eligible men she knew had no interest in raising another man's child. So how would she possibly find a man to raise two children?

She admitted that seeing the words *Child Advocate* etched on her office door at work saddened her most days. The irony was hard to miss. The hypocrisy almost incriminating. Nevertheless, she would do the only thing a woman in her position could do. First, she would decide that she must choose happiness over Charles Vargas. And then she would banish all thoughts of her unborn from her conscious mind. Far into the outskirts of her memory where neither she nor those guilt-ridden shadows of remembrance would ever find them again.

11

Not long after bedtime, Shadrack awoke to the sibilant sound of nighttime rain and a nagging telephone that wouldn't stop ringing.

"Syreeta ain't been home in four days, Shadrack," Zora Jones said through the phone. For the third time in a month, Syreeta had run off and left Asia.

"Where is she?" Shadrack said.

"Somewhere running the street." Zora Jones described the odd things that were happening lately. Twenty-dollar bills were missing from her purse, Syreeta was skinnier than a sewing needle, and different men were coming to the house late at night, which could only mean one thing. "She smoking something, Shadrack, and turning tricks to pay for it. I told her I can't be watching Asia like this. I got a life, too. She running them streets when she need to be home with her child. Now she all strung out."

Shadrack slowly sat up and sighed.

"You listening to me, Shadrack?"

"Yeah, I am," he said. "Where's Asia?"

"Right here 'sleep. Poor girl ain't ate since this morning. We been waiting on Syreeta to bring some groceries. Ain't no food in the house."

"I'm bringing some food right now."

"Never mind the food. Come get Asia. I need a break."

When Shadrack arrived in Kenfield to pick up Asia, Zora Jones was clapping fruit flies over the garbage can. Asia was wearing a pink raincoat, holding a Pound Puppy by the ear. "I'm calling the cops on your daughter, Ms. Jones," Shadrack said.

"And what they gone do, Shadrack?" Zora Jones said. "Ain't no need for that. Just find her. She can't be far. Try that man Felix, that hustler she know on the west side. He probably got her tricking over that way."

"You know the address?"

"Syreeta don't tell me nothing. Ask around. Somebody know him."

It was true. The next day, merely chatting with some folks at a self-serve car wash on Massachusetts Avenue yielded an address for a hustler named Felix. That wasn't his real name of course, but he was the one. If you needed base, he had it. Ecstasy, no problem. Weed, glitch, battery acid, he had it all. He stayed down the way on Plymouth Avenue near the liquor store. Green and white house at the corner. Knock three times, and he'll take care of you.

"What is it, son?" the man called Felix said, shielding his body with the door as he eased it open. He was holding onto the collar of a mean dog, and was frowning as if he perceived a bad smell.

"Syreeta here?" Shadrack said. He tried to peek past the partially open door but couldn't see much. Music was playing inside, and he could hear a couple of voices, but neither of them was familiar.

"I don't know you, son," Felix said.

"That's fine. I'm not here for you." The dog stirred a bit, as if it didn't appreciate Shadrack's tone. "You know where I can find her?" Shadrack said.

"I don't like your attitude, son. You might wanna step off before I let this pit bull bite the butt cheeks outta your ass."

"Look, I don't want trouble. I just need to speak to Syreeta."

"Syreeta not here."

"She left Asia again. Everybody's concerned."

"I told you she not here." The door shut before Shadrack could say another word. He had almost made it back to his car when the door opened again and Syreeta appeared.

"I'm right here, Shadrack. What's wrong?" She avoided eye contact, and her lips were crusty and white, her hair matted. The impacted dirt in her fingernails suggested she hadn't taken a shower in days.

"You left Asia again," Shadrack said.

"My mother got her."

"She's with me now."

"So what's the problem?"

"You need help, Syreeta. Who's this guy you're staying with? You should be home."

"Don't start acting like you better than me, Shadrack." Syreeta scratched at an itch in her arm, a vigorous scratch, as if she felt some multi-legged creature crawling under her skin. "What I do ain't got nothing to do with you."

"What about our daughter?"

"Ask yourself that question," Syreeta said. "What exactly do you do for her, Shadrack? Now that you trying to be father-of-the-year all of sudden, and you so much better than me, tell me what you do other than send a few pennies outta your pocket every month. You got a lot of nerve coming here butting in my business like I owe you an explanation when you ain't even my man."

"Are you tricking out here, Syreeta?"

"None of your damn business."

"Then Asia stays with me."

Syreeta gave another scratch to her arm and glanced back at the house when Felix hollered out her name. "Be my guest," she said, turning back to Shadrack. "We'll see how long that last."

Weeks later, when Syreeta hadn't returned home and hadn't inquired about Asia, Shadrack filed for temporary custody. Loretta, still opposed to any man taking a woman's child, blamed Shadrack for Syreeta's problems. Had he been a better father all along, Syreeta wouldn't be seeking comfort in drugs.

"You don't bring the white man into your family affairs," Loretta said. "If you got an issue with Syreeta, you go to her, not the white man. Who made you judge and jury over everybody? I'm warning you, Shadrack. Leave well enough alone, or you gone regret it. You never listen to me. That's your problem."

"I did go to her, Mama. It didn't help."

"Don't talk back to me!"

"I'm supposed to leave Asia over there while Syreeta's out tricking in the streets?"

"You don't judge," Loretta said. "Let God judge."

The judge, it turned out, was a middle-aged white woman who presided over custody cases at Erie County Family Court. She assigned a child advocate named Giselle Brooks to represent Asia in the case. Before conferencing with her, Shadrack and Loretta met with a lawyer that Shadrack had retained earlier in the day, a balding Jewish man who gave them tips on how to present their case. "Just be you, Shadrack," the lawyer said. "No reason to be uptight. She'll ask about your job, home life, family—those kinds of things."

"Shadrack don't have no family other than me," Loretta said.

"That's fine, Miss Ford. She just wants to know Asia's in good hands. Be sure to tell her how you go to church and everything. All that sounds good."

The lawyer's assurance gave Shadrack confidence, though the nervousness never subsided. Official matters intimidated him, and he feared he might say the wrong thing and ruin the case.

"Giselle is as good as they come," the lawyer added. "Her father was mayor. Remember Mayor Brooks?"

"I didn't know he had a daughter," Loretta said.

"She's great. You'll love her."

When Giselle arrived, she handed out handshakes, then showed everyone to her office. They sat around a conference table, discussing Shadrack's employment status and other issues related to temporary custody. Giselle sorted through a heap of documents and lifted several sheets to the top. "Well, I couldn't reach Syreeta," she said, "But her mother agreed to let Asia stay with you guys for now. I'll recommend temporary custody until Syreeta's in a better position."

"How long?" Loretta said.

"Really depends on Syreeta. Maybe six months. Enough time for her to get on her feet."

"We didn't have to come to court for that," Loretta said to Shadrack. "It's not right to take a woman's child."

"Well, if it got everybody focused on Asia's best interests, then it was a good thing," the lawyer said. He patted Shadrack on the back.

Giselle agreed. "I support your son's decision, Miss Ford. A lot of young fathers wouldn't care. We need more of them to start making a difference."

"A girl needs her mother," Loretta said. "After six months, then what?"

"We all get together and see where we are."

Before everyone stood up from the table, Loretta said, "I didn't know Mayor Brooks had a daughter. Or maybe I forgot."

"I usually stayed out of trouble," Giselle said, smiling.

"That was my house your brother ran into."

Giselle's smile faded. "*Your* house?"

Loretta nodded. "Ninety-nine Peach Street. The one with the garden."

Giselle examined a document in front of her, evidently surprised to have missed this detail, one that must have mattered greatly to her family once upon a time. Her bewildered gaze rose from the paper. "I see," she said. "Funny how small this city is." She escorted them out of the office into the courtroom. Her smile never came back.

12

The gash under Syreeta's eye was real and tore vertically from the high point of her cheek to her chin. She wore no stitches and no bandage to cover it up, but probably should have considering how badly Felix had cut her face. Apparently, she had ended their affair and told him she was leaving. This in itself was not a mistake, because anyone who knew anything about Felix knew that the last thing he respected was a woman. The mistake was choosing not to end it with a kitchen table letter or a simple phone call after she had already left. But for some strange, inconsistent reason, Syreeta had done things right this time, and told him face to face, only to lose part of hers in the process.

Unexpectedly, she had appeared in the doorway with bloodshot eyes that were sad and tired of something, and Shadrack, noticing the slice of anger on her face, figured now was not the time for discussing the past six months or asking a thousand questions about what Felix had done. It was time for consolation, which was what he gave her the entire time she remained at 99 Peach Street. According to her, she had once again reached a point where things had to change. She had a daughter to raise and a future to prepare for, which meant no more street running. No more tricking and getting high. No more slick men who valued nothing outside of the bountiful paradise of her spread-open legs.

So she took up residence there, and all was calm for a while. But it was still Loretta's house, and Loretta reminded Shadrack of that each time Syreeta talked smart—each time she refused to go to church or stood in the way when Loretta wanted to spank Asia for something. They fought all night sometimes, tossing furniture between them, hurling insults and threats so virulent Shadrack feared that one of those angry ladies would be the next soul laid to rest under that yew tree out back.

"Two women can't live in the same house," Loretta declared, finally. "Especially when the other woman is an ungodly heathen." Stone-faced, Loretta turned away from Syreeta whose presence, she said, she no longer acknowledged. "No more shacking up in my house, Shadrack," she said. "Pack her bags. Send her back to Kenfield."

"She'll take Asia from me, Mama."

"The heathen and her baby gotta go."

For this reason, Shadrack had no choice but to rent his own place, an apartment around the corner, not more than five minutes' walk. When Loretta learned his intentions, she cursed him and called him ignorant so many times Shadrack stopped counting.

"That heathen gone ruin you, boy," she said. "You wanna be some street hoodlum like her?" It was plain nonsense, according to Loretta, to go wasting money on some place around the corner when he could be helping her pay bills right there. "You done sniffed a little broth of manhood, now you think you know everything."

But Shadrack played deaf and signed the lease anyway. Upon leaving, he set down his bags and offered Loretta an embrace, but she stiff-armed him. "Walk out that door, Shadrack," she said, "and you'll never step foot in this house again. Understand?" She didn't blink. "When that hooker break you down, don't come here."

"Can you support me for once in my life, Mama?"

"If you walk out that door—"

"Do I always have to do what you say?"

"You'll never come back."

"Can I make my own decisions?"

"Walk out that door, Shadrack—"

"*Can* I?"

"You'll never step foot in here again."

"*Can* I?"

"Never again." Loretta still hadn't blinked.

For a moment, sensing his mother's coldness, Shadrack lost his nerve and reconsidered. The future frightened him. Uncertainty, snarling like a wolf, lurked in the shadows of it. For the twin bed upstairs was the only bed he'd ever slept in. And now, according to his mother, he'd be sleeping on the sidewalk long before he'd ever sleep in that bed again. But his love for Asia surpassed everything, and the dignity of fatherhood promised him more peace of mind than any familiar bed. So he had to do it. Blindfolded and handcuffed, he had to take the leap.

The apartment was a furnished bachelor on Orange Street that overlooked the black tar roof of Hassan's Liquor Store. An old-fashioned frumpy living space—mere space that served as evidence that one could not expect the world for the price of a month-to-month accommodation in the Fruit Belt. Space more suitable for a grandmother who raised cats, someone for whom the sour scent of old carpets and the sound of leaky faucets would have been bearable, because those things, just like old wallpaper and old-fashioned appliances, only appear old to young people, people who didn't exist when these old things were new—when a leaky faucet was a blessing compared to a backyard well, and when the sour smell of a carpet was merely the smell and consequence of having laid fabric on an indoor floor.

Syreeta dropped her bags onto the sofa bed and observed the surroundings. "This the best you could get, Shadrack?" she said. Shadrack watched her inspect the appliances and the kitchen cabinets, cabinets with doors that wouldn't snap shut. The shelves

were dusty and bare except for a box of stale cereal left behind
by the previous occupants.

"For now it's better than living with Mama," Shadrack said.
From a window wet with fog drip, he gazed skyward. Not a thread
of sunlight cut through the dense cloud cover above. And that
was how it felt inside the apartment that day, gloomy and
overcast. Shadrack, trying to lift spirits, made popcorn and hot
chocolate on the old double burner stove, and everyone sat on
the carpet watching reruns on a twelve-inch, black-and-white
television that had strips of aluminum foil twisted around the
antennas for better reception.

"How long we staying here?" Syreeta said.

"Until I save enough for a house."

"And how long that gone take?"

"Not too long."

But what didn't take long was the rebirth of Syreeta Jones,
and she was blunt. It had dawned on her, she said, that she stood
to gain more by leaving with Asia than staying there struggling
with Shadrack. Why stay when she could leave now and get
welfare, not to mention child support? She wouldn't have to
answer to him. Wouldn't have to depend on him for what she
needed, and live by his rules. If she left with Asia, Shadrack would
have to pay, and she could still get food stamps and WIC and live
life how she damn well pleased. Instead of staying and kissing
Shadrack's ass, she could wave farewell and make *him* do the
ass kissing. "So don't test me," she said.

Hearing all this, Shadrack grew suspicious, especially when
Syreeta wanted to take Asia to Kenfield on a Sunday morning
during church time. "Fine," he said. "You go. Leave Asia."

"What, you don't trust me with my own child?" Syreeta said.
"Who are you?"

"It's Sunday. She's going to church. Go wherever you want,
but she stays with me."

"I don't need your permission, Shadrack. That's my child. I'm taking her."

"Over to some pimp's house?"

"Wherever I go, she go. And if I take her to a *real man's* house, ain't shit you can do about it."

"Stop talking to me like that, Syreeta—"

"Or else what, Shadrack?" she said, raising her voice. "You gone run home to your mama? Good. Give her my regards."

"How about I shove those words back in your mouth—"

"Go right ahead, nigger, do it," Syreeta said. "'Cause I got 9-1-1 on speed dial, son. And while you locked up, guess what I'll be doing. I won't be sitting up in this raggedy motherfucker all night. I'll be going to see my *real man* who give it to me how I like it."

"Syreeta, if you don't stop disrespecting me it won't be the cops getting called. It'll be Mr. Niederpruem coming to pick up your dead body. That's no joke."

Syreeta raised her middle finger to his face and inflamed in him a desire to pummel her the way Loretta would have done to him when he was younger. This was his first inclination. The second was to walk out and leave that finger suspended there, aligned in the cross-eyed vision of no one, which is what he did. But when he returned from church, Syreeta and Asia were gone, and he could not find them.

13

Every day was trash day somewhere. And each garbage bin was packed to the lid with cash. Aluminum soda cans, that is. Bottles and things. Money foolishly discarded and waiting for some indiscriminate garbage truck to carry it away. A whole five cents per can, which was real money for anyone not too proud to collect it. Why couldn't she simply gather the cans and bottles from the garbage bins herself, then pack them into a couple of rusty shopping carts, and lug them all the way to the supermarket to redeem the cash? Over a month, perhaps, she could make up some of the income she had lost now that her son was gone.

At the end of the second week, a package had arrived from him. An envelope with some money. But not a lot. At first, Loretta thought to flush the envelope and its contents—both the cash and the contrived sympathy—right down the toilet bowl. But toilet water couldn't defray the cost of lights. Nor could it cover the cost of groceries. Shucks, toilet water itself cost money. So she chose not to flush it, for every little bit helped when she put it with the cash she earned collecting cans and bottles from trash.

Tears rolled when she calculated the price of her son's absence from her home—the absence of his salary at least. She had told him never to come back mostly because she didn't know what she would do without him there, without him helping her with those unceasing monthly bills. After all this time and all these years,

Loretta still didn't have enough. Still couldn't get a better job and survive alone. Still, even after all this time and all these years, she hadn't mustered enough money even to get a simple porch railing fixed. Couldn't borrow the money because she'd never earn enough to pay it back. Wouldn't dare ask the insurance company, because they'd want to know who the hell she was living in Mattie Turnbull's house.

So it had to be cans and bottles. Five cents for each one. Simply gather them from every trash bin she could find. Because buried among all that stinking rubbish was the clean pristine scent of money—of lights and groceries. Water she could drink and flush. All the simple things required to make life livable. What Shadrack sent every other week wouldn't be enough. But again, it helped. She depended on it. Needed every tiny bit she could get from wherever she could get it. So one could understand her desperation when Harold Niederpruem called one morning saying he might have to find someone else to do Shadrack's job. He hadn't heard from him in several days, and received no answer when he stopped by his apartment. He didn't think Shadrack would quit his job without telling him, so maybe something bad had happened. Nevertheless, he had a business to run. The decision wasn't final, but he might have to let Shadrack go permanently if he didn't hear something soon.

Wearing slippers, a housecoat, and a head full of pink rollers, Loretta trotted over to Shadrack's apartment. "You gone lose that job, Shadrack," she said. "You hear me, boy?" Shadrack lay in bed, blanketed to his neck. "I done had enough of you and that silly girl. Now if it was up to me, I'd let you lay there and die. But we need you to keep that job. So get up." Loretta tried to shake him from his misery. He shooed her away and rolled over. She tugged at him again. He didn't budge. "Shoulda listened to me before," she said. "You can't fix no worldly woman. What you expect was gone happen?" Loretta whisked away the cover and hurled it toward a heap of dirty laundry on the floor. He was wearing only a pair of white briefs and socks. "Do you hear me talking to you, Shadrack?" she yelled. "Do you?" If her son needed sympathy, it would have to wait until after payday. The nerve of him to be here malingering while she was out collecting cans and bottles every day just to avert starvation. She found a leather belt and whipped him out of the bed.

"Stop it," he said. "Stop. I'm up."

"Then get clean. Do it quick."

A pile of unwashed dishes stank up the apartment. As Shadrack showered, Loretta washed them all and took out the garbage. She cleaned the counters and gathered the dirty laundry from the floor. Shadrack had no clean clothes, but there was no time to worry about that. He would have to wear dirty ones.

"I need to find Syreeta," Shadrack said, emerging from the bathroom.

"Forget her," Loretta said.

"I have to find Asia."

"When she's older, she'll find you." Loretta dressed him in smelly clothes and led him by the hand to the front entrance of The Blessed Home. "Listen to me, Shadrack," she said. "I've been depressed before. Lord knows I understand. Sometimes bad thoughts be sprouting up in your mind like chickweed. You gotta keep plucking them out. Keep your mind stayed on Jesus, and you'll have peace. In any case, you can always get another woman. You can always have another baby. But you can't always get a good job. Mr. Niederpruem is a good man to let you come back. Don't mess up. Get in there."

"I feel like dying, Mama."

"Be a man!" she snapped. "I shoulda never let you hang around that Brother Gilbert. Bow your head, Shadrack." And with her palm to his forehead, Loretta spoke in tongues and prayed against every last demon of depression.

Into the back corridors of The Blessed Home, Shadrack followed Harold Niederpruem down to the basement where the air was damp and fusty, and flecks of black mold had stained the walls. The body of an elderly woman lay on a table down there, arms at her sides, a rubber block elevating her head. Shadrack put on a pair of latex gloves and helped wash her body. Harold Niederpruem sprayed disinfectant into her ears and nose and told Shadrack to plug them while he secured the eyelids and teeth with cement.

"Hard work keeps a man's mind off his troubles," Harold Niederpruem said. "When I was a young man, before I met my wife, I fell for an Irish girl down in the First Ward there. Real pretty girl, hard to recall her name now. Anyway, people married young in those days, and when you got engaged, you followed through with it. But her parents didn't approve because I wasn't Irish, you see. So they took her away. Just disappeared. Still don't know where. All to get her away from me. She never even broke off our engagement. You can imagine how I felt. Kind of wanted to give up on life, just like you. But I didn't. I only worked harder."

Shadrack nodded.

"See, in my world, a man is measured by that, as he should be. If he doesn't work hard, he's not a good enough man. He's not respected. He has no say. In fact, the way I see it, the worse you feel, the harder you should work. You can't change people, Shadrack. All you can do is work harder."

But Shadrack failed to heed this advice, and things began to slip away. After hearing a rumor that Syreeta had gone to Rochester with Felix, Shadrack made the ninety minute drive and searched for them. He had no choice. He had to find Asia. He couldn't let his daughter grow up to be somebody's whore. He drove down every street, road, and avenue. Cruised by every bar and street corner, desperate for a chance sighting of Syreeta, perhaps out on the stroll hailing tricks. But he never found her. He checked every school district in the area to see if Asia's name popped up on some school's attendance record. But it never did. Then someone said it was Detroit and not Rochester. So Shadrack drove back six hours the other way. Still nothing. Someone else said Felix did business in Charlotte sometimes but that maybe it wasn't smart to go driving all the way down there blind. Ignoring them, Shadrack journeyed south for twelve hours until he reached Charlotte, North Carolina. Still no luck.

"Did you ever consider Canada?" another person said. "Sometimes pimps take their hoes up to Toronto. Lots of money being made up there."

It was a long, painful trip back north. He steered twelve hours back to Buffalo and crossed the border at Fort Erie, then drove two more grueling hours toward the bright beautiful skyline of Toronto, Ontario. He searched every street and street corner. Every rooming house, hostel, and hotel, and only gave up when there were no more areas on his map to search.

When he had spent weeks driving across states, city to city, street to street, exhausting every dime of the money he started with, Shadrack returned to Buffalo with nothing but a quarter tank of gas and frail nerves, and he figured he may as well go back by Zora Jones's place and start again. Kicking at the door, he demanded to be let in.

"Stop kicking my goddamn door, Shadrack," Zora Jones hollered from the other side. "Syreeta ain't in here."

Shadrack kicked some more and pounded his shoulder against the door.

"I got a gun, Shadrack," Zora Jones shrieked. "Now get on outta here, you crazy nigger."

"I'm going to kill her when I find her!" Shadrack yelled. "I'll burn this place down." When he couldn't get through the door, he threw rocks and tree limbs at the front window. Then a garbage pail; and then, finally, a brick, which shattered the glass completely. "I know she's in there. I want to see my daughter." But before he could climb through the shattered window, the police were already on the scene, restraining him. Shadrack flailed about so hysterically he struck one of the officers, causing her to fall and break her arm. He thus received a free ride downtown to the Erie County Holding Center where the magistrate wouldn't let him go without substantial bail. Criminal vandalism was bad enough, but assaulting an officer of the law constituted a grave offense. Moreover, the magistrate entertained no discussion of Asia, because such a family issue should be dealt with in family court.

When Loretta refused to post bail, declaring that they couldn't afford both freedom and a lawyer, the county moved Shadrack to the correctional facility in Alden, which became, at least until the trial, his new home. This was just as well, because by then he had already lost his apartment, his job, and apparently his mind.

14

For Audwin Brooks, at age thirty, all of life was the struggle for mornings of uninterrupted sleep. So when his parents bullied him into a series of temporary jobs, arguing that the sun should never rise over a sleeping man's face, and that this—working instead of sleeping—was what a grown man should be doing with his life, Audwin concluded that life itself (if what his parents had said was true) was devoid of all real purpose. Because no matter what anyone said, work was nothing more than a rhetorical swindle, a wicked euphemism for purposelessness and bondage, devised only to make poor people proud of doing something they hated to do. Had not hard labor been the oppressor's tool of subjugation against his ancestors? Yet now his parents spoke as if it was somehow liberating to show up to some workplace every day and grovel for the very same money they (or any one of his girlfriends) could simply leave next to the unplugged alarm clock each morning while he slept.

In other words, slumber represented the highest order of freedom, especially for the black man. Thirteen decades after Emancipation, the simple stubborn privilege not to work was his reminder and assurance that he was still free—that he alone was the arbiter of his Destiny, come what may. Moreover, the suggestion that any form of fulfillment could unveil itself before saggy, sleepy eyes was pure myth. Because when you think about it, of all the things in life that gratify the human soul, the only thing anyone really desires is a little more sleep, a little more freedom. And as far as Audwin was concerned, if life equated to freedom, and freedom equated to sleep, then living meant sleeping until three-thirty in the afternoon.

Nevertheless, his parents forced him to work, and he did. After sleepwalking through a number of factory jobs, sales jobs, and even some street sanitation assignments, and then quitting each after only a few days, he settled on working as a security guard at the Olmstead School, a private school on the north side of town. He worked Monday through Friday, eight hours a day, from 8 a.m. until 4 p.m., patrolling entrances and hallways and making sure students didn't cut class or hang too long in the lavatories. He monitored the detention room, kept order in the cafeteria, and assisted any teachers who had disruptions in their classrooms. It was a simple enough job for now. Nothing much ever went wrong at Olmstead. Most of the faculty members were competent and laid-back, and the students generally treated everyone with respect. But it was temporary employment, not to be confused with something he'd do forever. Eternal fulfillment lay only in the dream side of consciousness. Long naps and slobbered on pillows. Snoring. Waking up and passing out again. Freedom.

Most of the time, he worked alongside a man named Pritchard Jennings, a modest, shovel-nosed fellow of considerable girth, who had been doing security at Olmstead twelve years already, and was apparently so delusional about the nature of pride and happiness that he had become enthusiastic about his own enslavement. Each morning, with an annoying smile, Pritchard was first to greet students as they filed into the building.

"Morning, youngsters," he would say. "Y'all ready for a good day?"

With springs in their steps they would answer, "Yes, Mr. Jennings. All ready for a good day."

"Behave yourselves now. Make your parents proud." And before any of the students sprang away to their classrooms, Pritchard would incline his shovel-nosed face toward Audwin. "Youngsters, aren't y'all forgetting something?"

"Good morning, Mr. Brooks."

Audwin would mumble a perfunctory good morning, though to him no morning was ever good unless you were just now heading to bed after drinking and copulating with a good-looking woman all night. Not that a man like Pritchard Jennings would know much about that. In fact, he seemed to know nothing at all, and lurched into an elusive silence whenever the topic of women came up in conversation. He had no stories to tell. No bragging. No hilarious accounts of wining, dining, and dumping some immaculate church girl right after her first sexual experience. Audwin had already decided that Pritchard was gay until they were having lunch in the break room one afternoon and Pritchard finally broke his silence.

"So, Audwin, I've been thinking," Pritchard said. "You talk a lot about women and stuff. I wondered if you could introduce me to a nice lady. I mean, you're probably saying 'what the heck a big, grown man like that need help finding a woman?' Well, it's a long story. I won't bore you with the details. But it's been like ten years now —"

"Say what!" Audwin said, almost knocking over his soda. "Ten years since what? Since you had sex?"

"Well, I don't know, I guess you could say that."

Audwin stared at him.

"It's complicated," Pritchard said. "Don't get me wrong, I've had a woman here or there. But I usually end up not doing anything because I'm a little shy about my issue."

"If you have a problem getting it up, they have treatments."

"No, not that. I mean, I'm sort of, well . . . *ineffectual*."

"Ineffectual? Pritchard, what the hell are you talking about?"

"Maybe I'm not using the word right —"

"You mean you can't please her?"

"No, not that either." And then he explained how he would never be a father. Although he worked well with children and had a rapport with them, he could have no children of his own. No doctors had told him this, but they didn't have to. Because even at age forty-two, not a single offspring (legitimate or illegitimate) had come forth to disprove people's suspicions that he was walking around hopelessly empty. Women left him when they discovered this emptiness. And he lamented how his beloved wife had divorced him ten years ago and made babies elsewhere with a man whose loins effervesced with life-giving possibility. "So, that's why I don't get involved too much," he said. "Kind of hard when they just leave you like that 'cause you can't have kids."

"Let me get this straight," Audwin said, dying to laugh. "You can get the woman. You can get it up. But you can't get her pregnant, so you don't bother."

"Pretty much," Pritchard said. "I don't want to embarrass myself. Lot of women don't respect a man if he can't produce. I thought maybe you knew somebody who didn't have expectations . . . kind of looking for an ordinary fellow like me."

And this, Audwin came to learn, was actually the most remarkable thing about Pritchard Jennings, that he was, in fact, a pathetically ordinary man. Humble and nice, but not particularly interesting on any front. Because for him, life was a simple pastime. Sure, everybody had ups and downs and shortcomings, but if you worked every day and came right home, paid your bills on time and went to bed early, things had a way of becoming predictable. And he liked that. He took few risks and lived life at a bargain. While others used their paychecks to buy cars and clothes, he held onto his money like blood and lived happily within his means. He could save up enough cash to buy a Lincoln, but he preferred to drive a Hyundai instead. No law precluded him from wearing Polo and Ralph Lauren. Many people did it. But Goodwill clothes were just fine with him. The Olive Garden Restaurant tasted delicious. He expressed no doubts about that. But what was wrong with Denny's and their blueberry pancake special on Saturdays?

Ordinary. The kind of man who told a bland joke and expected you to laugh, and glared at your face until you did. A single woman's consolation prize. The best she could get at the time. A safe bet. Not the loser of the race. Not the winner. But that guy in fourth place. The kind of man who took his own popcorn to the movies. Invited a woman for a walk in the park, not to be romantic, but to avoid paying for a real date. Commonplace. Dull sex. The same-old-same-old. Thrifty. Plain. Childless and ordinary. Naturally, then, it was through pure dumb luck he came to marry Audwin's sister, Giselle, the daughter of the former mayor.

It was during this time that Eric, Audwin's nephew, was attending Olmstead. Each morning, Giselle would drop him off, and then wave to Audwin and Pritchard on her way out. Both would wave back. Pritchard's wave would last longer.

"She makes you wish you'd dressed better today," Pritchard said once as Giselle passed by and out of the main door.

Audwin was seated at the security desk and looked up from his automobile magazine. Pritchard's eyes looked as if someone had waved a magic wand in front of them. "Get real," Audwin said. "Women like her don't want guys like you."

"Obviously," Pritchard said. "But she's beautiful. Seems like a wonderful person."

"Don't be too impressed. She's just Giselle."

"What do you mean?"

"I mean stop gawking at my sister, asshole."

But the next day, as Audwin read his magazine and Giselle passed by with her usual wave, Pritchard gawked again and said, perhaps, the only thing he could have possibly said to make the miracle happen.

"I see Eric like a son," he said. "All these kids are like my children."

This time when Audwin looked up the magic was in Giselle's eyes. Apparently, that stupid comment had touched her somehow and made Pritchard Jennings, instantly, a very lucky fellow. Because he just so happened to be the most ordinary man in the world at the very time Giselle needed someone ordinary to take the zing out of life, to suck all the unpredictability out of it. A man, she said, to simply hold the damn wheel and drive straight. Don't make her guess where they were going. No more surprises. No more unexpected turns. Something slow and steady. Something boring. Something ordinary. The polar opposite of Charles Vargas. And by elimination that left a man like Pritchard Jennings.

One morning, after Giselle dropped Eric at his classroom, Audwin pulled her aside and into the security office when Pritchard wasn't around. "What kind of game are you playing, Giselle?" he said. "People say you've been dating this dude. What is this?"

Giselle rolled her eyes. "You're making me late for work, Audwin."

"Come on, you know you're not interested in Pritchard."

"He's nice. Maybe I am. Are you my chaperone now?"

"I'm your big brother."

"And he's your friend, so stop stabbing him in the back."

"He's a coworker, not my friend."

"Well, you'd best get to know him better then."

"This is a joke," Audwin said. "I can't believe this. What are you going to do with a man like Pritchard Jennings?"

"What's wrong with him?"

"He's a security guard."

"So are you."

"Only temporarily."

"I don't care," Giselle said. "I think he's nice." She explained that her days of chasing perfection were done. If this simple, ordinary man with the heart of a true father was good at all, then by

God, he was good enough. Nothing had come of the wealthy men, even less of the pretty ones. And now, at twenty-eight, raising an adolescent boy without a father, she had decided against chasing images of the perfect man. She needed an *actual* man. A husband and a father, whether perfect or not. Of course, some security guard named Pritchard Jennings wasn't the man of her dreams; she knew that. All of Buffalo knew that. But he wanted to marry her and be a family, and that mattered.

"So when he proposes, I won't refuse," she said, throwing her chin in the air. "It's time to take control of my life. I just need to convince Mother and Father of it, and then, I guess, once again convince myself."

When Giselle formally announced her engagement, Bernadine convened a family meeting, urging everyone to slow down. Pritchard Jennings hadn't been invited. Audwin was irritated that he himself had to be there—that anyone had to be there—when his spoiled brat sister had obviously made up her mind, and couldn't be swayed. Everyone was seated in the family room, everyone seated except Bernadine who stood before Giselle, pleading her case, rambling on about how, yes, Pritchard Jennings comported himself as a reasonable, well-mannered man, but that Giselle had only known him a few months, and these days, no one married anyone after only a few months. Besides, Bernadine said, Garrison women had always observed a four seasons' policy. You had to know someone through all four seasons, and all holidays, before even thinking about marriage. For what it was worth, Audwin had his own four seasons' policy. Never entertain a woman for longer than a year. She might have a four seasons' policy.

"It's a new generation, Mother," Giselle said. "We do things differently now."

"Now hold on, Bernadine," Cornelius said, chuckling. He sat with his arm over the back of the sofa. "Your family didn't think I was good enough either."

"You find this funny, love?" Bernadine said. Frustration mounted on her face. "This has nothing to do with being good enough. She's rushing this thing. Can't you see that?"

"She's twenty-eight. If she doesn't know what she's doing by now, we can't help her."

"That's not good enough, Cornelius," Bernadine said. "You can't up and marry somebody you barely know."

"You really plan to marry this guy, Giselle?" Cornelius said.

"Yes, Father, I do."

"Good luck trying to stop her, Bernadine."

"Audwin?" Bernadine said, sounding desperate for an ally.

Audwin shrugged. He wanted a drink. The very saliva in his mouth tasted of gin and juice. He would head to Birchfield's the moment his mother stopped wasting everybody's time trying to talk a single woman out of marriage. He had once seen a bride with a broken ankle march herself to the altar with a cast and crutches. Even heard that a Cheektowaga couple once exchanged vows in a recovery room at Mercy because the groom suddenly required an appendectomy the morning of the scheduled wedding. But he had never known mere words to forestall an eventuality so inevitable that nothing short of an earthquake could stop it, if even that. In any case, he voiced his opinion. "Yeah, I'm with you, Mother. It's crazy."

"Finally," Bernadine said.

"Audwin, you're just jealous," Giselle blurted out. "Everything I do, you have a problem with it. You don't like Pritchard. That's all it is. That's why you quit that job."

Having not yet told his parents about his decision to abandon his temporary enslavement, Audwin should have expected that Giselle would embarrass him. She hadn't changed much over the years. "Fine," Audwin said. "Marry that big-nose idiot. What do I care? Who's jealous?"

"Admit it, Audwin. You hate for me to be happy. You've always hated it. Well, I don't want to be miserable like you."

"Miserable?" Audwin said. "Miserable?"

"You quit the job, Audwin?" Cornelius said.

"This is about me now, Father?"

"Actually, Audwin, it's supposed to be about me, if you didn't know," Giselle said.

"Why don't you kiss my ass, Giselle—"

"Enough, enough!" Bernadine hollered out. Cornelius stood, as if he might need to protect his daughter from his son. No one said another word. And that settled it. A wedding happened. Giselle and Pritchard were married. An ordinary ceremony with the same old people. Same ordinary songs everybody sings at weddings. The usual vows. The normal line dances at the reception. His spoiled sister had what she wanted. She had ordinary. She had boring. By God, she had Pritchard Jennings. What Audwin had, however, was an assurance that this sham marriage was already doomed. Because hearts don't change much over time, and if he understood anything about a woman who had loved hard before, it was that the wraith of a lover long gone visited her in dreams, and almost always returned in the flesh.

15

On a sweltering Saturday in July, around noon, Audwin (having been persuaded by Pritchard to spend some time patching things up with Giselle because "Brother and sister shouldn't quarrel like that," and because "Afterward, me and you can get a couple beers, my treat") agreed to ride with Pritchard, Giselle, and Eric to the east side to pick up Pritchard's ten-year-old niece, Keesha, who lived in the Kenfield Projects with her mother, Pritchard's sister. Pritchard had been born and raised in this part of town. Many of his family and friends still remained. He recounted a funny story of his father, a bitter old man who lived by himself on Oakmont Street in Kenfield, and owned a gun, a revolver, though he never showed it, except to scare away the neighborhood gang bangers with Polaroid pictures of it that he kept taped to his front door.

"Don't the gang people have guns, too?" Eric asked, sitting in the back seat with Audwin. Giselle, wearing sunglasses, glanced over her shoulder for a second but said nothing.

"Some," Pritchard said. "But they don't mess with folks who can shoot back."

"Why do they want to shoot people?"

"Not everybody's out here shooting people," Pritchard said. "Things just get a little overheated sometimes. Nobody's going to shoot you, I promise."

"Did your dad ever shoot anybody?"

"Eric . . . " Giselle said, again glancing over her shoulder.

Pritchard laughed. "I hope not," he said. "No, I don't think so. My dad's a nice man. A little grumpy, but that's because he's been around a long time. Takes a lot to get a smile out of someone who's seen it all. Tell you the truth, I don't know if he really has a gun. That photo could be from Guns & Ammo for all I know."

"Maybe you should be his bodyguard like you do at school."

"You mean security guard," Pritchard said. "Me and your uncle are security guards."

How complicated all of this had to be for young Eric. Some man, some shovel-nosed substitute for a father, moving in and changing up stuff overnight. All along, Eric and his mother had been living in the peaceful seclusion of a condominium on the seventeenth floor of the Nottingham Residence. The complex stood on Cedar Grove Crescent, a narrow cul-de-sac off North Sussex Avenue in North Buffalo. Now that Pritchard Jennings had moved in, and had apparently committed himself to giving the sheltered young man an unfiltered glimpse of the "real world," Eric had to be feeling a little uncomfortable, if not irritated.

"Don't worry, nephew," Audwin said, reaching over and patting him on the head. "Mind your own business, nobody will ever bother you. Don't take anybody's money, don't get caught in bed with their woman, you'll survive anywhere."

"He's fine," Giselle said.

"Just schooling my nephew on life."

"Women and money are not life, Audwin," Giselle said. "He'll manage without the street-smart survival tips, okay?"

"We said no quarreling today, guys," Pritchard said.

"We're not quarreling. We're talking," Giselle said.

Other than that, Giselle hadn't said much. She seemed calm, but it was hard to tell how she really felt about all of this. After Catholic school, North County High School, the University at Buffalo, and its law school, she had married herself into a world her entire upbringing had structured her to avoid. And now it was hilarious to watch her flailing and flopping in an awkward skydive back to earth, and pulling her son down too. Being cool about life's possibilities was noble. Their mother had always taught them to be good citizens, compassionate, concerned about those who have less. But this—this world of projects and ghettos, gangsters and guns, and some plain old slumber party masquerading as a marriage—this was the wilds. Giselle was a domestic cat. Proud product of the black bourgeoisie. Not the housewife of some ordinary working-class guy for whom slogging his way out of Kenfield amounted to success beyond all expectations. Oh, the humble desperation of the single woman, the single mother such as Giselle, who, compelled to barter away her self-respect for the semblance of family normalcy, could no longer accommodate her own inborn over-particular tastes in men, but now had to close her eyes, point somewhere, and then open them to see who her husband was going to be.

The young girl Keesha insisted on going to Roosevelt Park near the projects instead of Delaware Park in North Buffalo as everyone had planned. She wanted one of the free lunches community workers gave out around noon. Even when Giselle suggested hotdogs from Leo's over on Colvin Avenue near Delaware Park, Keesha still preferred to get a free lunch. Today they could be serving her favorite: peanut butter sandwiches (actually peanut butter mashed between two graham crackers), which happened two or three times per summer, and she didn't want to take a chance on missing it.

When Eric heard this, he said, "My grandfather said there's no such thing as a free lunch."

"That's not true," Keesha said. "Me and my friends get one every day. Don't you get a free lunch at school?"

"No. My mom pays for it."

"Whoop-dee-doo," Keesha sang out, whirling her finger. "Good for you." Her mother had done her hair nicely with braids and beads, and had dressed her in sun-bright yellow shorts and a white blouse that had pretty butterfly embroidery on the front of it.

"Ain't nothing wrong with free lunches, Eric," Pritchard said. "Don't make Keesha feel bad."

"He's not trying to make her feel bad," Giselle said. "He's just not used to this."

"What do you mean?"

"Give him some time to get used to things."

Pritchard left the car in the projects, and they crossed into Roosevelt Park via a footbridge that arched over the Kensington Expressway. Young Keesha led the way, carrying a can of bubbles and a kickball. Eric dribbled a basketball behind her, clumsily, as if it were his first time. Giselle followed them, wearing a backpack cooler full of popsicles and barrel-shaped Huggies drinks.

"She got anything in that cooler for a grown man to drink?" Audwin said to Pritchard.

"If she did, I doubt she'd give you any."

"That's the truth."

Roosevelt Park was wide-open and green with very little shade and a redbrick shelter house at the rear, just before an area of high grass. Some kids were assembled there, and the community workers were already cutting open the cardboard boxes and dispensing plastic-wrapped lunches. Today each package contained a bologna sandwich, a raisin cookie, a banana, and a miniature carton of two percent milk.

"What about peanut butter sandwiches?" Keesha said to one of the community workers.

"Not today, sweetie," he said. "Bologna is better for you anyway." He stayed attentive to the eager reaching hands that had swarmed to his newly opened box. He bent over and pulled out four lunches at a time, two in each hand, and doled them out. Most of the children, many of them with their mothers or older siblings, grabbed their lunches and trooped back over the footbridge. Some of them sat on the ground by the shelter house, eating, sometimes trading items amongst themselves, or pilfering from a child who was distracted. Keesha took her lunch and sat down with some of her friends.

Pritchard nudged Eric. "Go get a lunch."

"I don't eat bologna."

"Some kids don't have a choice what they eat."

"Leave him be, Pritchard," Giselle said.

"A boy can't go through life thinking he's better than other kids."

"It's not that."

"Then what is it?"

Giselle shot him a wooden smile. "It's not a big deal, Pritchard."

Audwin surveyed the bright green landscape. Aside from the community workers and the children at the shelter house, the only other people in the park was a group of shirtless teenage boys sprinting across the basketball court, shooting into crooked hoops that had no nets. At the other end of the park lay a tennis court, but it likewise had no nets, and ragweed grew from the cracks in its surface. When Audwin noticed the splash pad and inquired about its strange lack of water on such a hot day, Keesha said there never was any water as far as she remembered. Pritchard concurred and said he couldn't recall seeing any water in it except when it rained.

After Keesha finished her lunch and tossed the wrapper into the garbage bin, everyone walked away from the shelter house. They high-stepped through the area of high grass, which was waist-high and itchy, and each of them scratched at their sweaty arms and legs, and swatted away flies.

"They should cut this grass," Eric said. "Weeds make me allergic."

"That's what we forgot, your allergy medicine," Giselle said. "Oh, Lord."

"Is this a ghetto park, Mother?"

"Don't say that, Eric," Giselle said.

"There's nothing wrong with this park," Pritchard said. "Start complaining and we're going home."

"Fine with me," Eric said.

"That won't be necessary," Giselle said.

As they walked, Pritchard pointed to a football field off to their left. Much of the middle was worn to dirt, and three of the orange pylons that marked the end zones were missing. "That's where I used to play football as a kid," he said. "Right there." The armpits and collar of his Hawaiian shirt were soaked.

"I didn't realize they played football back in that century," Audwin said.

"Funny," Pritchard said, but he didn't seem particularly amused. It couldn't have been because of the harmless quip. Audwin had always picked the scabs of Pritchard's insecurities. Most times, the man seemed to like the attention that a cooler, younger guy was giving him. His current ill humor must have stemmed from a gradual recognition of what Audwin already knew: Giselle Brooks was a handful, and Eric was the other hand full. What a mismatch of identities this was. Giselle Brooks, daughter of the former mayor, locked in a marriage with some school security guard from the projects named Pritchard Jennings. Their worst days were ahead. It served them right, though, especially Giselle, who still got away with everything. Had Audwin done something so capricious, Father would have had him flogged and pilloried before a lynch mob at Niagara Square. But life had a way of correcting injustice. And Audwin enjoyed watching every episode of the unraveling.

Near the picnic shed, Giselle handed the kids Huggies drinks and popsicles. Afterward, she and Keesha chased bubbles, popping the floating globules in mid-air, and then played a one-on-one game of kickball on the baseball diamond.

"Wanna go play basketball?" Pritchard said to Eric.

"All the rims are messed up."

Pritchard stared at him. "I told you to stop complaining, or I'm taking you home."

"Fine, take me home."

"You remind me of a spoiled two-year-old," Pritchard said. "You need a spanking."

"Chill, Pritchard," Audwin said. "Everything's cool. We'll hang out here."

"You're not my father," Eric said. "You can't tell me what to do."

Pritchard grabbed Eric's upper arm. "I'm better than your father," he said. "A father is the one who takes care of you, not the one who runs away. So watch your mouth."

"Chill out, Pritchard," Audwin said. "Let him go."

Eric yanked his arm away.

"Pritchard!" Giselle yelled from the baseball diamond. She rushed over. "Did I see you put your hands on my son?"

"He's being disrespectful."

"No, I wasn't," Eric cried.

Giselle latched a hand to her hip and held up a finger. "Let's get something straight. Never put your hands on my son, ever."

"I didn't hurt him. I disciplined him."

"Well, don't discipline him then."

"How am I supposed to be his father, Giselle?"

"You're not his father. He already has one."

"So, what am I?"

"You're Pritchard. I thought we understood that."

"Last time I checked I was the only father he knew."

"Eric knows his father. And you don't need to talk to me like that, especially when you live in a place where I pay all the bills. Or did you forget that part?"

"That apartment is my home, too."

"Yeah, but I gave you a reason to be in it."

"What are you saying?"

"Figure it out."

Pritchard walked off in the direction of the basketball courts. Keesha was still at the baseball diamond, kicking around her kickball.

"Thought we weren't supposed to be quarreling today," Audwin said.

"Shut up, Audwin," Giselle said. "The nerve of that man."

Audwin shrugged. "Thought you married him so he could be a father to Eric."

"He's not my father," Eric said.

"I don't go for people putting their hands on my child. I don't care who it is."

Audwin shrugged again. "I'll go talk to him."

He caught up to Pritchard halfway to the basketball court. The man was sweating profusely, breathing heavy as if Giselle had sent him away running.

"She's always doing that," Pritchard said. "Since we got married, all she does is put me down. She don't want me to ask where she's going. Don't want me to say anything to Eric. I never felt so bad about myself before. I'm an ordinary guy. I'm not used to folks thinking they're better than people. We're all human beings, you know."

"Yeah, I know," Audwin said.

"When I moved into the Nottingham Residence her neighbors treated me like I was a talking monkey. I tried to be friendly, knocked on a few doors. They acted like something was wrong with me, like I had some kind of scent I couldn't wash off, or a great big Kenfield sign branded on my forehead. Maybe I smiled too big or spoke too loud, but that don't make me a monkey. Where I come from folks don't turn down friendship without knowing you first. They sure don't judge you off the way you look. So then, guess what Giselle said. She said I was being a dummy and imagining things. Get that. Day after the wedding—the day you move in—and your new wife call you a dummy."

"I wouldn't take it personally," Audwin said.

"How am I supposed to take it?" Pritchard said. "Now Eric wanna say I'm not his father. Every day I bring him home, help with his homework, make dinner, play video games. Don't that sound like a father to you? But I don't fault him. He's a boy. Giselle should teach him to respect me, good as I been." He expelled a few more heavy breaths, as if talking that fast in such heat was strenuous. "You're her brother," he said. "What should I do?"

"Man-to-man," Audwin said, "if it was me, I'd let her go. But that's just me. I'm a bystander."

"Lord knows I love the girl. I'll do anything for her."

"How's the sex life going?"

Pritchard's eyebrows shot up. "I shouldn't be telling you that."

"Ever seem like her mind's a hundred million miles away?"

"Well, yeah, but I figured she's still gotta get used to me."

"Never initiates anything, always makes you wait hours before you get it?"

"Yeah, well, what does that mean?"

"Means exactly what you think it means."

"You saying she's still in love with her ex?"

Audwin nodded. "She can fool everybody, but she can't fool me. Don't let her fool you either."

Pritchard started whimpering into his hand. Audwin watched him for a few moments, thinking that too many men cried these days. Every television program and radio. Every sporting event and wedding. Every politician and movie star. From everywhere, an endless chorus of weeping men. Who had rung the bell that commenced all the world's men to crying at once? Blubbering fools, persuaded by some talk show host, some quack therapist, that nature had gotten it wrong, and that the answer was simply to shake off that burdensome male machismo and just cry about it. But no woman could ever bring Audwin Brooks to tears. No, not him. He knew better. Male weakness didn't bring the humanity out of a woman. It emboldened her and hastened the day you walked in and found some naked, dry-eyed gigolo affixed to her backside.

"Naw," Pritchard said. He wiped away tears with his collar. "We have our problems, but she's a good woman."

"Better watch your ass, my brother."

"Naw, I trust her."

"A lot of guys trusted her. Watch your ass. With Charles Vargas, you don't stand a chance."

"Why are you telling me this, Audwin?"

Audwin went silent. After Pritchard uttered his name again, Audwin said, "Because I know Giselle. I know how she's making you feel."

Sweet gin was a proper solution. But he had only one way to get it. And if these folks couldn't tell the difference between young and old then perhaps he was justified. The grayness of his father's hair was not ambiguous, nor was the time-honored familiarity of the name anything less than a bell rung right at the ear. But these bankers, this teller in particular, was either unaware or didn't care, or it had been too long of a workday already, and a glass of gin would be her solution as well when she got home. Too caught up now in the hustle of an afternoon rush to be circumspect about things. It's not easy to be thorough under pressure, he supposed. Sweet gin must be beckoning her, too. And she could probably dream of nothing else but getting it.

"How much, Mr. Brooks?" the auburn-haired bank teller said when Audwin showed his father's ID. And he conjured an amount large enough to matter but too small for Father to notice upon checking his extra account, which thankfully was seldom, because this was all rainy-day money, stashed and forgotten. Squirreled away for some family emergency and for days that required a big blue bottle of gin to get through. Sweet like honey, or the taste of water when the sun is high; the touch of a woman when you feel so low. A mere drop, even a drop, could add some meaning to this miserable thirty-first birthday of his.

A while ago, he learned that his mother would no longer be cooking him dinner. Sure, on Sundays there would be enough food for everyone. But only because it's Sunday, and everyone gets food on Sundays. The rest of the week he had to fend for himself. Screeching vacuum cleaners woke him in the early mornings now. Shower water went cold after only a couple of minutes. His girlfriends called, but no one gave him the messages. Anytime he used the house phone, Bernadine suddenly had more important matters pending and needed him to clear the line. Whenever she found him napping or playing video games, she made him take out the trash or mow the lawn or transfer storage bins to the garage, only to lug them into the house again once she'd changed her mind. It never failed. The mere appearance of contentment spurred his mother to find some reason, some petty chore, to upset his day.

The liquor store wasn't far from the bank. Middlesex Road wasn't far from the liquor store. All was quiet when he arrived home. Bernadine had baked a cake. Colored and pretty but not large. Lemon was his favorite. Round and yellow with white trimming, waiting on the dining table with a birthday card. He hadn't expected much. His birthday never stood prominent on the family's calendar of events—the cake being a mere perfunctory acknowledgement of it, a grudging acceptance of its inevitable arrival every twelve months to the day.

With his mind yet sweetened by gin, he wended toward the sound of television. His parents were cuddling in the den, watching an episode of the Cosby Show. One of the characters made them laugh. Before the smiles subsided, Bernadine said over her shoulder, "We think it's time you move out, love."

For a moment, Audwin assumed he misheard her, or that those words were not hers at all. Too much gin might do that. Make a television voice sound like that of his mother. When he realized it was no hallucination, he said loudly, "Say what? Move out, why?"

"Have you any plans for your life at all?" Bernadine said.

"I'm finding a job, Mother. You guys know that."

"Yeah, but you'll quit after a few days and stay unemployed for months," Cornelius said. "You're thirty-one, Audwin. All you do is hang out late partying. Staying here rent-free won't help you grow up. It's time to get your own place."

"We're taking you off our car insurance too," Bernadine said. "You have to get your own policy."

Audwin let out a roar. "I can't believe this. You hate me that much?"

"Nobody hates you, Audwin," Cornelius said. "We'd be less than parents to let you keep living like this."

"But I can't afford my own place, Father," he said. "Mother?"

"Maybe you can take up with one of those girlfriends of yours," Bernadine said. "Might be good for you. I know it'll cramp your womanizing a bit . . . "

"Why should it? It never cramped Father's." Audwin let out another roar. He kicked the door and stormed to the dining room where he fetched the lemon cake. He carried it back to the den and slammed it to the floor. The cake squashed at his parents' feet, flattening into a yellowish-white mush on the carpet.

"Audwin!" Bernadine said. "What's wrong with you?"

Cornelius had to restrain him from cutting up the furniture with his switchblade. Bernadine, dashing behind him, had to stop him from smashing her china against the walls. Audwin flew to his car with nothing but his video game console and some clothes. His endless roars invited all of Middlesex Road to the drama. "I hate everybody in this family!" he hollered. "You'd never do this to Giselle, you assholes!"

Swerving onto the main road, he sped straight to the house of a woman named Reniyah Stroud, a girlfriend of his, a grade school teacher with a good salary and a refrigerator full of food. She wasn't his favorite girlfriend, but these were desperate times. Forced to choose which woman to live with, he had to select the one who could care for him best. The one who could afford those big blue bottles of gin. Father would discover the thievery soon, so there would be no means to get it otherwise.

The matter was therefore settled. It would be Reniyah Stroud. Not his favorite. But she would do for now. When he arrived at her place, he barged in without a word. And then, with perhaps too much force, he took her down and entered her. It was not love. It was not sex. It was rage. And he gave her every last bitter ounce of what he had.

17

Bernadine heard the screams. Giselle came rushing back into the house, her boots tracking snow into the entranceway. "That man is crazy, Mother," she said. She had left a few moments ago after a short visit, but somehow hadn't made it out of the driveway and was now back inside, bolting the door.

"Who?" Bernadine said. "Pritchard?"

"Yes, it was him."

"Where is he? That son of a bitch."

"He ran off," Giselle said. "Oh, Mother. He scared me." A week ago, she and Pritchard had fought over Charles Vargas. The fight ended with Pritchard hurling her into a bookcase. Bernadine had insisted on reporting it to the police, but Giselle said no. She didn't want anyone knowing her business, not even her father. Instead, she kicked Pritchard out and told him it was over. He hadn't stopped calling since the breakup, and in recent days had left no fewer than a hundred messages, though Giselle hadn't returned any of them.

"You don't have to be scared, love. What happened? You want me to call the police?" Cornelius wasn't home, and no one had heard anything from Audwin.

"He was there," Giselle said. "He scared me."

"Did he do anything to you?"

And Bernadine could hardly believe what Giselle told her next. That a minute ago she had gone to her car, and Pritchard slid from under it, begging to know if Charles Vargas was the real reason she kicked him out. That was when she screamed.

"I can't think. I can't sleep," Pritchard had said. "Please don't leave." He was shivering. Snow was all over his clothes. "Please, Giselle."

"I have nothing to say to you," Giselle said, stepping back toward the portico.

"I didn't mean to hit you, I swear."

"That's the last time that'll happen. Now leave."

"Did you sleep with him?" Pritchard hurried to block the door. "Please. You can't throw me away like this. I wanna know why you married me if you still loved him."

"I used to love him, Pritchard. I *used* to. It's not the same now."

"But it is true, right? Be straight with me." He reached for her.

She jumped back. "Stay away from me. Do I have to call the police?"

"Just tell me!" he yelled.

"Yes," she yelled back. "I still have feelings for him. Is that what you want to hear? I hope you feel better, because I don't. I'll probably always have feelings for that man, and God knows I'm sorry about it. But it's not about him now. It's about you and what *you* did."

"So it's true, you had sex with him?"

"Leave," Giselle said, and let out another screech. Pritchard darted away down Middlesex Road, leaving a trail of footprints in the snow.

Bernadine felt the need for a Valium. A man so disturbed that he would lie down in the snow under a woman's car was capable of anything. She had always suspected something was unbalanced about him. This confirmed he was completely unhinged. "I'm calling the police right now," she said. "That's enough of this."

"No, Mother, don't. He didn't hurt me."

"Why are you letting him get away with this?"

"I feel sorry for him," Giselle said, starting to break down. "He doesn't look well at all."

"Stop feeling guilty. You didn't do anything wrong. He knew about Charles from the beginning. He's your son's father for Christ's sake—" Bernadine was about to say something else when Giselle interrupted her.

"I went to see Charles again, Mother," she said.

Before Bernadine could reason a response, Giselle told her about the phone call she received. She was in a meeting. At first, she ignored it. But he kept calling, and she found it difficult not to yield, difficult not to wonder where he'd been and what he wanted. She excused herself from the conference room and took the call.

"Hey, it's me," Charles Vargas had said.

Giselle hung up and waited for him to call back.

"Nothing to say to me?" he said when she answered again. "I want to see you."

"You abandoned us, Charles."

"I had some issues to work out. I thought about you, though. Thought a lot about Eric."

Giselle made him listen to dead air. She could have transcribed this much of the conversation before it happened. She had no reason to think the rest would be new.

"Heard you got married," he said. "You must be real glad."

"It's not a good time, Charles."

"I have something for you."

"So I should drop everything because you say you have something for me?"

But in fact, she did. And amid the revival of the old obsession, it was impossible to hide from Pritchard the fact that something had changed. And this brought on the arguments, which led to the silence, which provoked the fights, and that was when Pritchard hurled her into the bookcase.

Infidelity. Throughout the generations, this word hadn't entered the family lexicon. Bernadine felt no sympathy for Pritchard Jennings, but she had taught Giselle better, the way she herself had been taught. The way all Garrison women had been taught. Though she had prepared to make an exception for divorce (an annulment because the couple hadn't observed the four seasons' policy anyway and because a man who would hit her daughter deserved no place in their family history) no excuse could be made for infidelity. Why, love?" Bernadine said. "Why would you do such a thing?"

Giselle sobbed in her arms. "I shouldn't have married him, Mother," she said.

"That's very true, dear," Bernadine said. She rubbed her back. "We all make mistakes. Time will take care of it."

"Can I tell you something else? I don't want you to get upset."

"I don't need to know everything, love."

"When I was out there, something else Pritchard said. He said it was Audwin who told him I was seeing Charles. Would he do that?"

"If he did, he won't see tomorrow."

18

In the upstairs bedroom of Reniyah Stroud's house, Audwin reclined in a wicker chair, naked with his bare feet to the warm carpet. The thermostat was set to eighty-five degrees, as per his request, keeping the room toasty, so that the frost on the dark windowpanes had softened and melted away. The room was so warm that the medley of jolly Christmas songs playing on the stereo began to seem grossly out of season, especially since he hadn't bothered, for many days and nights now, to venture out into the cold December air. Reniyah's kidney bean smell filled the room the way it always did whenever she removed her panties. She was showering now, but that did nothing for the unbending odor in the air, a smell that only reminded Audwin how bland her sex had become. She had gained so much weight, and the ever-present kidney bean smell only worsened with each layer of fat she put on. Moreover, he could swear her insides felt different now. Loose and vacuous with a recurring frigidity he found immensely frustrating.

Reniyah emerged from the bathroom in a bra and panties and rummaged through her dresser for a turtleneck, and then a pair of jeans, which were difficult to button around her ballooning waistline. "You going to sit there all night like that?" she said. "Shower up so we can go somewhere and celebrate."

"It's ice cold out there," Audwin said.

"Christmas Eve is always cold," Reniyah said, sucking in her gut to fasten her jeans. She folded down the collar of her turtleneck, then palmed her breasts and bobbed them into place. "We can hit the Elmwood Lounge. They've got Lance Diamond on tonight."

"Nah," Audwin said. "Fix me something to eat."

Reniyah placed a hand on her broad hip. "And then what, you go to sleep? Well, I won't be here when you wake up. You never take me anywhere. All we do is screw, screw, screw. I don't want to be cooped up in this house all night."

Audwin's head fell back over the rim of the wicker chair.

Reniyah Stroud was twelve years his senior, an established woman with a suburban house, benefits, and a salary that increased every year as long as she remained a teacher with the Buffalo Public Schools. Recently, now that Audwin resided at her home full time, Reniyah had begun to ask questions about their future as a couple. But each time, Audwin answered the same way. He wasn't sure yet, because maybe he wanted to have children and she was already over forty. Moreover, marriage wasn't something he thought about much, or even considered important, much less useful at this point in life. So their affair proceeded as usual, as if there were no endpoint and no deadline. No urgency or expectations. Each day no less ambiguous than the day before.

Reniyah went to prepare Audwin a sandwich, which she brought back on a saucer. She held a gin and tonic in the other hand. "Here you go," she said with an edge. "Enjoy."

Audwin guttled the sandwich. Gulped most of the gin. Belched, farted, and then said the first thing that rattled in his mind. "You know, I'd kill a bitch if she cheated on me. Everybody said Giselle was so much better, so perfect. Now they know the truth."

"How do you know she cheated, Audwin? You weren't there."

"The whole world knows she cheated."

"Well, everything you hear ain't gospel. You shouldn't have gotten involved."

"If somebody fucked my wife, I'd want to know."

"Not every man is like you. Anyhow, last time I checked, you didn't want a wife."

"Whatever. All I'm saying is I'd kill a bitch . . . "

"Shut up about killing people. I don't want to hear that crap."

When Audwin asked what she would do if someone cheated on her, Reniyah stated her philosophy with the eloquent, common sense tone of a schoolteacher. Basically, you get fifty years in jail for killing someone. So simply wait fifty years. If you still hate the person after all that time, by all means kill them. If not, at least you didn't go to prison for something you'd regret later.

To that, Audwin added nothing. "Don't worry. I wouldn't hurt you, Reniyah," he said.

"But you're a jealous man. What's to stop you from going crazy? Ought to be ashamed of yourself going behind your sister's back. Your parents must be pissed."

"Fuck my parents." He threw up his middle fingers. "All they care about is Giselle. Fuck her too."

"You really feel that way about your family?"

"Do they give a shit about me?"

"Why wouldn't they?"

"They'd never put Giselle out in the street."

"You're not in the street, Audwin. Don't be melodramatic."

"That's not the point, Reniyah."

"Then maybe there *is* no point, Audwin." She went to start the shower. When she came back, she clutched his wrists and hauled him from the chair, telling him to take a shower and stop being so mean.

After dialing Reniyah Stroud's house and getting no answer, and then trying repeatedly to catch Audwin on his cell, Cornelius slammed the phone onto the base and turned to Bernadine. "I can't reach him."

"He's just avoiding us."

"He can't get away with this, Bernadine."

"He won't," she said. "But you shouldn't get so worked up. He'll surface eventually. Then we'll deal with him." Not only had Audwin betrayed his sister and destroyed her marriage, he had stolen thousands from the family bank accounts, which everyone now knew. Even tried to steal again recently, but a vigilant bank teller grew suspicious, alerted her manager, and exposed the fraudulence before Audwin could get another dime.

"I should go over there right now," Cornelius said.

"Go where, love?"

"That woman's house. I know he's over there."

"And what will you do, my dear?"

"I'll knock him out, that's what."

"You're talking about our son, not some street hoodlum."

"A beating is long overdue for that boy, Bernadine. I should have knocked him out a long time ago. We wouldn't have this problem. He's nothing but a drunk, and probably on drugs too."

"He's not on drugs, Cornelius. Let it go. Wait until you cool off."

"No," he said. "I'm his father. It's time to teach him a lesson."

"Too late for that, my love. Much too late for that."

That same night, Bernadine headed down the snowy thoroughfares of North Buffalo, past Delaware Park and Route 198, up Main Street and Michigan Avenue, until at once the roads narrowed, and she was toiling through the unplowed streets of the Fruit Belt. It was after ten o'clock, and the shops were closed, and she could barely tell the abandoned houses from the lived-in houses as her headlights guided her through the rugged, snow-obstructed byroads that led to 99 Peach Street.

Bernadine's boots trudged through mounds of unshoveled snow up to the house. Grasping the crooked railing, she mounted the porch stairs and pressed a cold finger to the doorbell. A woman in a flannel nightgown peeked out the window, then opened the door to the chime of a jingle bell wreath that hung there. For so long, Bernadine had envisioned someone older, a woman her own age perhaps with graying hair and aging skin. But Loretta Ford, she now realized, was at least ten years younger than she, standing behind the storm door, curious, sipping from a mug of something warm even as Bernadine shivered in the falling snow.

When Bernadine identified herself, Loretta pushed open the storm door and stepped aside. "Have some hot chocolate?" Loretta said, taking her coat and showing her to a seat.

"I wouldn't dare take up so much of your time," Bernadine said. "I hope you'll forgive me for coming uninvited. Turns out my whole family has had a chance to meet you except me."

"Well, I think y'all have too much interest in a simple woman from the Fruit Belt," Loretta said. She grinned cordially. "But I don't reckon you came all this way just to make my acquaintance. What can I do for you?"

This house, 99 Peach Street, with all of its meanings and histories, was practically noiseless, dark with a monastic quietude common to homes not often visited. The living room was lighted by a wall-mounted lantern, and the smell of cinnamon wafted up from a tray of incense, like the sweetness of Christmas bread baking, only commingled with the faint scent of ashes and a curl of smoke. Aside from that smell and the sound of the jingle bell wreath that had greeted her on the way in, Bernadine perceived no signs of the Christmas season, and she simply deemed Loretta Ford one of those introverted people not given to the holidays, or perhaps one who had sad memories attached to the season and chose not to celebrate.

"Seems like yesterday," Bernadine said. "I worried so much when Audwin had that accident. I never thanked you for helping him. That was impolite of me, to say the least. Despite our differences, I believe all mothers see eye-to-eye when it comes to the safety of our children. So, if I offended you by not coming here before . . . "

"That's quite a ways back, Mrs. Brooks."

"It's never too late to make things right."

"You would have done the same for my son."

"Of course," Bernadine said. "Of course I would." The bleakness of the outside air lingered in her fingertips. She sensed heat in the house, but it was turned down low, too low in fact for the coldest night of the season so far. And it occurred to her that people with less money probably had to worry a lot about their utility bills. "But to be frank," Bernadine said, "I'm not sure I would have been so quick to divulge what happened here that night. Nothing's been the same for us since. Might sound strange, but it's true."

"And you think I'm the one who told?"

"Didn't you?"

Loretta set down her hot chocolate, looking pensive, and apparently, whatever she was contemplating had to be reached for and hadn't been summoned in a long time. Quietly she said, "A woman's secrets hide in a dark and lonely place."

"I beg your pardon?" Bernadine said.

"That's what Mattie Turnbull used to say."

"I don't follow. I'm sorry."

"Years ago, I loved a man back in South Carolina," Loretta said. "When I came to Buffalo, I was heartbroken, depressed. Then I fell in love again, and that man let his friend rape me in my own home." She paused and reached back into her mind again. "But you see, I was brought up not to complain—that maybe sometimes we bring misfortune on ourselves. I know you know what I mean. All the crap they say to women when men abuse us."

Bernadine affirmed it with a nod.

"That thing hurt me to my heart. Hurt me forever. But even after that, when I barely felt like living, I never said a word about it to anyone. Not a soul. Never once. So when you ask me, Mrs. Brooks, if I'm the one who brought down your husband and shamed your family, I want you to consider the secrets I've already kept and ask yourself if you really think I'm the one who told."

"My God. You poor woman. I can't imagine."

"It wasn't me who told on your husband."

"One of the neighbors, perhaps?"

"Nobody else came here that night."

"I see," Bernadine said. "Nobody except Audwin."

Silence ensued. Loretta reached for her hot chocolate again.

"When I came here tonight, I knew," Bernadine said. "But I had to hear it from you. Otherwise, I would've never accepted that my son would do so much to destroy his family. I just don't know why he would do it."

"Can't understand everything, Mrs. Brooks. Some stuff we gotta go to our knees about."

Bernadine rose and slipped on her coat. "Thank you," she said. "I won't take up any more of your time." At the door, she turned back. "By the way, whatever became of that man you loved?" she said. "The one here in Buffalo."

"I won," Loretta said coldly. "He been dead six years now, and I'm still living."

19

The problem was not that his younger sister was smarter. He could live with that. He didn't aspire to be smart anyway. It wasn't even that she was destined to be somebody greater than he'd ever be. He had already come to terms with that too. The problem was that everyone, including his father, knew those things without a doubt. Giselle made their father proud. He didn't. She would be successful in life. He wouldn't. Indeed, by the mere force of her existence, she spotlighted his mediocrity before the one person he wanted to please most. Rudely, overtly, she had become heir to their father's dreams, while he, Audwin, was the trademark symbol of their father's shame. No question about it. Giselle was his favorite. And if it were, instead, something of a quiet approval stored in the innermost lock box of the man's heart, it would have been no issue. But he, Father, approved openly and divided his love in a way that showed everyone where he stood. In particular, he seemed unsurprised by Audwin's shortcomings. Indifferent to the missteps. Unmoved when he brought new disgrace upon himself and his family, as if nothing more was expected in the first place, and that he, Father, had already accepted that his son's salvation lay far beyond anyone's prayers or reach. And what could be more insulting than that?

He was a young boy when all of this first occurred to him. His parents had arranged for him and Giselle to recite speeches at the annual Easter celebration sponsored by their neighborhood church. Parents and children had gathered in the sanctuary. His sister went first.

"Giselle, honey, they're ready for you," Bernadine said, scooting the young girl up to the podium. She didn't need her paper. Confident and flawless, she recited the speech from memory, undaunted by the faces in the audience. Then it was Audwin's turn. He carried his speech to the podium but only stared at the words on the page. After a few silent moments, he dropped the paper to the floor and bolted from the sanctuary in tears. When his mother found him and brought him back to his seat, Audwin could sense his father's shame like a scent from the man's body. Having been eager to make his father proud, he had practiced for weeks. But at performance time he failed, unable to recite the speech from memory or read it from the page. Because reading was hard for him. And it made him sad that his father thought he was stupid.

But of all the events that came back to him at times, fourth grade at the Olmstead School was the most vivid. His teacher was a gum-popping spinster named Miss Turner, who had no family and talked endlessly about her four dogs.

"Come in students," she said on the first day of school. Twelve students rushed in and plopped down at the desks. "That's not how we do it here. I want you all to try again."

They lined up outside the classroom door again and waited.

"This time you'll enter silently without running. As you can see I have desks on that side for boys." She pointed to one side of the room. "And desks on this side for my lovely girls."

The five boys and seven girls entered and took their seats.

"You'll also see another one in the back." She pointed to a lonely desk in the coatroom. "That one is for bad kids."

Audwin had no reason to expect he'd ever end up there. He had never been in trouble with his other teachers. In fact, he rarely uttered a single word in class, trying to conceal his disability.

What the other kids could do he simply could not. They memorized scores of spelling words and read aloud in front of the class. But he couldn't. Words made no sense to him. Letters shifted on the page. And it didn't take long for Miss Turner to notice.

"Audwin, I'd like you to read for the class," she said. She stood before his desk, cradling a textbook in her arms. "Start at the top of page fourteen please."

Audwin looked at the page. A sudden acceleration of his heartbeat seemed to swirl the letters around. He twitched his head and batted his eyelids, hoping this would halt the frantic movement. But it didn't.

"Do you have fleas in your head, Audwin?" Miss Turner said.

Audwin heard the snickers of his classmates. Again, he stared at the pages, shook his head, batted his eyelids. But the letters only circled faster. So he just gave up and recited, on pitch, a singing exercise he once heard on Sesame Street.

"Me and Mario! Me and Maria. Me and Mario! Me and Maria."

The laughter exploded in his ears. Miss Turner scowled and plunked her book onto his desk. "You clown," she said, leaning forward into his face. "This is the Olmstead School. Your classmates are here because they're special. They're smart. Not just because their father is running for mayor. You'd better start acting like you belong here, young man. Go sit in the coatroom right now."

Which he did for the rest of the day, did for much of the school year in fact, because whenever his teacher commanded him to read, he couldn't do it, and proceeded to sing his song instead. Each time he did this, Miss Turner devised some new way to punish him.

"Give me your lunch box," she said once. "You won't be eating with the other students today." During lunchtime, while the other students ate in the cafeteria, Audwin stayed in the classroom with Miss Turner. "I've had enough, Audwin. Take out your reading book. Starting today, you'll read if you want to eat."

Audwin opened his reading book and stared at the page.

"Open your mouth!" Miss Turner yelled, startling him in his seat. "Read it. And do it right. If you sing that stupid song, you're getting a paddle." She held her yardstick near his face.

After glancing at the yardstick and then his lunch box, Audwin returned to the page and uttered, "T-The…"

"Good," Miss Turner blurted out. "Finally, we're getting somewhere." She opened his lunch box and tore off a piece of his sandwich. "Here you go." She tossed it onto his reading book. Audwin picked it up and ate it. "Okay, now read some more."

"T-The…"

"Read it, Audwin."

"T-The…b-ball…"

"Good. Here you go." And she tossed another piece onto the reading book.

After that, Audwin would have nothing more to eat that day because he could go no further, and Miss Turner, not willing to reward him for repeating the same two words over and over, discarded everything his mother had put into his lunch box. He went without a full lunch for weeks before he threatened to tell his parents.

"Tell them," Miss Turner said. "Please do. I want them to know exactly how bad their son is."

So, of course, he never told his parents, because he couldn't bear his father being disappointed again.

"In fact, why don't I tell them myself?" Miss Turner said.

"No," Audwin said instantly. "Please."

"I'm sorry, did you say something?"

"Please don't tell them."

"All right. But if you speak to me like that again, I will. Don't forget it."

The terrible hunger led him to start eating his lunch in the mornings before school. When Miss Turner asked what he had done with his food, he was silent, and she ordered him to remove his shirt in front of the class. Standing behind him, she raised the yardstick.

"Now say it," she said.

And he said what she had warned him he would have to say if this ever happened. "Please give me a paddle, Miss Turner," he said.

"Again, louder."

"Please give me a paddle, Miss Turner."

And she burned his back with three lashes of her yardstick. Audwin sank back into his seat, sobbing, and could once again hear the laughter of his classmates. No longer did he eat his lunches before school. Each morning he surrendered his full lunch box, knowing Miss Turner was expecting it.

"It better all be here," she would warn. "Or I'll tell your parents. And you know I will, don't you?" He would nod and make his way to the lonely desk in the coatroom without having to be told where to go.

Eventually he began to steal coins from his mother's purse to buy snacks, which he would consume before school so he wouldn't get so hungry at lunchtime. But it didn't take long for Bernadine, a woman who kept good track of her money, to realize what her ten-year-old son was doing.

"He's rebellious," Bernadine said to Cornelius. Audwin could hear them whispering outside his bedroom door. "He's stealing now. Do something about it, love."

"How much did he take?" Cornelius said.

"I've noticed money missing from my purse the past couple of weeks. Maybe a couple of dollars every day, I suppose."

"A couple of dollars? Why not give it to him so he doesn't have to steal it?"

"That's not the issue, Cornelius."

"What is he spending it on?"

"I have no idea. He's still denying it. And that's not the worst of it. I spoke to his teacher yesterday. She says he's causing a lot of trouble. Says he's smart-mouthed and lazy and clowns around in class. I don't know what's gotten into him. Maybe you should spend more time with your son, love."

Audwin pressed his ear now to the door.

"How much time I spend with him has nothing to do with it, Bernadine. He's a boy. That's what they do. Part of growing up. He'll be all right. Now stop bugging me about these petty things."

The following week, Miss Turner told her students they would be practicing their uppercase letters in cursive. It was an individual assignment, and she would be checking their work when she came around. After demonstrating on the blackboard, she noticed that Natalie, one of the brighter girls in class, had gone into the coatroom to help Audwin. Miss Turner approached them, tapping her chalk-covered palm with the yardstick. "Natalie, did I tell you to help him?"

"He doesn't know what an uppercase letter is."

"This is an individual assignment. Go back to your seat." Then Miss Turner said, "Audwin, write for me an uppercase letter A. It's the first letter of your name. Do it now."

Audwin took hold of his pencil but did nothing with it. Having no idea what to do, he had only reached for the pencil because he was certain that was the first step in the process.

Miss Turner cocked her head. "Did you hear me Audwin? I said write an uppercase letter A."

"I don't know how."

"Do you know what an uppercase letter is?"

"No, Miss Turner."

Miss Turner gathered a notepad and marker from her desk. "Come with me, Audwin."

She left an aide with the other students and escorted Audwin down to the school basement where Mr. Fred, the head custodian, sat napping in his office, his feet on the desk, a boogie-woogie blues station playing on his transistor radio.

"Mr. Fred." Miss Turner rapped on the open door. "Mr. Fred."

"Yeah," he said, jolted from his sleep. When he saw who it was, he yawned, and then muttered in response, "How you doing there, Miss Turner?"

"Not good, Mr. Fred. Audwin here insists on making a buffoon of himself in class. He thinks he doesn't have to cooperate because of who his father is. So, I've decided to put him in the old janitor's closet until he's ready to come back to class. Do you mind?"

"The janitor's closet?" Mr. Fred said. He rose from his chair, gazing at the shamefaced young boy. "Well, I don't have time to be babysitting—"

"It's only for a short while, Mr. Fred."

"How short?"

"An hour or so. If he learns his lesson sooner, he can come back sooner."

But the old janitor's closet, Mr. Fred reminded her, was not a room they used anymore aside from storing junk. No one had had a chance to clean it out yet, and it was freezing cold, because the radiator no longer worked.

"Good. Even better."

"I don't know about that, Miss Turner. How about he sit in here with me? When I make my rounds, he can come and do some chores—"

"The janitor's closet will be fine, Mr. Fred. Audwin needs some time alone to reflect on how to be a better student in my class."

"You checked with Principal Mahler on this?"

"Principal Mahler says I can do whatever's necessary to make sure these children learn and behave. Now if you'll open the door please, Mr. Fred."

The old janitor's closet was right down the hall. Mr. Fred jangled his mass of keys until he found the right one, and then opened the door and flipped on the light. In the cramped room, a storage cabinet took up much of the space, standing about six-feet high, about as tall as Mr. Fred who entered first. He uprighted four push brooms that were strewn across the floor, and then discarded a stack of molded gloves that hung on the rim of a tarnished slop sink. "We don't be having kids down here like this, Miss Turner."

"Duly noted, Mr. Fred." Miss Turner nudged Audwin forward. He toddled across the threshold and started shivering. A bitter draft whistled through an air vent somewhere, or through some hidden crevice in the wall, making the room as frigid as the winter air outside, icy and cold, as if he had been brought there to preserve his flesh from spoiling. Moreover, the air was fetid, reeking with the odor of sour mop heads, one of which stood soaking in a pail of black water, a sight and smell so gross Audwin's stomach would have spewed its load were it not already empty and sore from hunger. Behind him, he heard the voice of his teacher.

"I'll need a desk for him, too, Mr. Fred. That shouldn't be too much trouble."

Mr. Fred got in touch with one of his guys by Walkie-Talkie, telling him to bring a desk down to the old janitor's closet in the basement, a request the other custodian found odd but fulfilled nonetheless. After it arrived, Mr. Fred returned to his office, and they could hear him plopping back into his chair and clunking his feet onto the desk. "You too hard on these kids, Miss Turner," he called out.

"Thank you, Mr. Fred. Sorry for disturbing you." Miss Turner positioned the desk so that Audwin's back was to the door. Then, uncapping the marker and releasing its inky fumes into the air, she wrote in big bold capitals the words THE UPPER ROOM on a sheet of a paper, though Audwin could not understand what it read. She taped it to the wall, securing it on all four sides with masking tape, so that now it had the likeness of a framed picture.

"You know what that says, Audwin?"

Audwin wobbled his head no.

"It says the upper room. Any idea why I'm putting you in the upper room?"

Again, he didn't know.

Miss Turner tore another sheet from her pad and set it before him with a pencil. "Very simple. You're staying here until you show me an uppercase letter A. The longer it takes, the longer you stay. You understand me?"

Audwin nodded.

"So as of today your father's our new mayor," Miss Turner said. She drew close to his face. "But that doesn't mean *shit* in my classroom." And Audwin turned in his seat to watch as she backed out of the room, shutting the door behind her.

When he was finally alone, Audwin tucked his head in his arms and wept from the bottom of his little soul. For the next three mornings, as he entered the classroom with the other children, Miss Turner singled him out, asking him to write an uppercase letter A. When he couldn't, she escorted him down to the upper room. The purple sign still hung like a framed picture on the wall. Audwin shivered from the cold and cried each time she left him behind.

Days turned into more days. Those days turned into weeks. And no new lessons happened because he still hadn't learned how to write his uppercase letters. Each day he merely doodled some formation of symbols Miss Turner wouldn't accept. "Can you show me how?" Audwin would ask.

But she would not. "It's an individual assignment. The longer it takes, the longer you stay in the upper room."

On and on it went, day after day, week after week, until one day around lunchtime, Audwin heard the door of the upper room creak open. He turned to see who it was. "Father?" he said with a touch of hope, a sudden gladness that warmed his spirit even though his body felt cold. But it was not his father. Only Mr. Fred, standing in the doorway, staring at him with the look that aging people sometimes have when they've grown suspicious of their own minds, as if he'd arrived and found a gymnasium instead of a janitor's closet, and couldn't fathom how it got in there without the key.

"Boy, your teacher still bringing you down here?"

Audwin nodded. "I can't write my letters."

"Because you can't write letters?" A bewildered expression. Like that of an aging man who could have sworn he'd bought two heads of cabbage instead of one and could find neither the cabbage nor the money he would have used to pay for it.

"Yes, sir," Audwin said.

"What exactly she want you to write?" Mr. Fred approached, glancing at the sign that read THE UPPER ROOM.

"Uppercase letters," Audwin said. He showed him a page of squiggly symbols and explained what his teacher had told him to do.

"Uppercase letters?" Mr. Fred's calloused hands took hold of the paper. He skimmed it briefly then gave it back. "Did she bring you any lunch?"

Audwin shook his head.

"She didn't even bring you no food?"

"No I didn't," Miss Turner said, standing in the doorway behind them. "I'll handle this, Mr. Fred." A tense exchange ensued outside the door of the upper room, an exchange of words Audwin couldn't fully hear, or at least in years to come he wouldn't remember. He remembered only what Miss Turner said when she turned and told him what she really thought of him.

"You'll never amount to anything, Audwin. Doesn't matter who your father is. By the time you're seventeen you'll be in Attica Prison."

But at seventeen, Audwin was more of a teenage rebel than a convict and skipped school about as often as he attended. He could read and write things now, but it remained a chore, and he absolutely avoided reading in public. Though older now— bolder, more confident—the memories of Miss Turner's class were vivid in his mind, and that part of him was still ten years old.

But despite the rebellion and the vulnerability, Audwin had become popular in his junior year at North County High School. He was tall and handsome and had little trouble getting girlfriends. They were willing to fight over him. When Jasmine Wilson found out that Rhodesia Cole had made out with Audwin in the back seat of his new car, she attacked the girl in the second floor hallway before homeroom. They scratched wildly. Clawed and headlocked each other before a throng of ballyhooing schoolmates.

"Apparently these girls were fighting over you, Audwin," Mr. Monticello said during a meeting in the principal's office. Jasmine Wilson and Rhodesia Cole were fuming.

"And?" Audwin said.

"Are you sleeping with both of these girls as they claim?"

"That's privileged information, Mr. Monticello."

"Not when it causes problems in my building, smart ass."

"Can I go now, Mr. Monticello?"

"If you spent more time in class than you do with girls you could go somewhere in life."

"I want the money you owe me," Jasmine Wilson blurted out.

"I'm not giving you a damn thing," Audwin said, and he exited the principal's office all set to find new girlfriends.

Though Audwin made many friends at North County, the best of them was no longer a student there. Silk, as everyone called him (a young man who had once played defensive end for the North County Bulldogs the two years they won the regional championship), was a high school dropout who bagged groceries at Top's and was the only teenager in Audwin's world who rented his own apartment. He lived in the McCarley Gardens, one of the poorest areas of town, which in itself made him one of the most interesting people Audwin knew. Because unlike many black youth in Buffalo at the time, he had chosen this life for himself. His parents were actually well off, his father a dean at Canisius College, his mother one of its most esteemed professors. Adoptive parents, and this was no secret, because no one believed that a young man with honey-brown skin had been born naturally of two white parents. And though he had been afforded all the benefits and accoutrements of an affluent suburban upbringing, he wished to discover his true identity. For he knew nothing of his biological parents, didn't know their names or ages, and had no hint of how they looked save for the fleeting glimpses of resemblance in his mirror image.

Silk's passion to unearth his biological roots superseded any desire to be counted among the starched white collars of suburbia, and led him during his coming-of-age to reject everything his privileged life had represented. He started getting high and drank himself into stupors so profound he once woke up in a dumpster somewhere on the east side with nary a clue how he ended up there or how long it had been. He dropped out of school, moved to the city, and joined the Nation of Islam, denouncing some of the very people and privileges that had nurtured him his entire life. In other words, he rejected his artificial whiteness. Rejected his parents and their love and did the opposite of whatever would make them proud. It made sense to him. In order to learn the truth about himself, he had to oppose those things that had blinded him to who he really was.

Now Audwin, in his own search for identity, admired Silk's rebellious approach to life. Being confronted with his own problems—controlling parents who favored his sister, nagging administrators who threatened to expel him from school—he found Silk's defiance rather appealing, and he longed to be like him. To seek after *Allah* for guidance and truth, and to experience the enlightenment that marijuana brought. To curse out his parents, and to fuck girls, and to shove a big black foot up society's ass and leave it there. This was what Silk represented. A true identity for Audwin Brooks. The freedom to bury his past, and to slap the shit out of Miss Turner if he ever saw that bitch again.

Destiny had brought Silk into his life. Literally. Because he and Silk had only met because they discovered they were both unknowingly dating the same girl, Destiny Hodges, a cheerleader at North County. Each assumed he was her only boyfriend until Silk found Audwin's number in Destiny's purse. After some macho blustering through the phone, the two boys decided it made more sense to confront Destiny and not each other since she was, after all, the one telling all the lies.

They confronted her together at the homecoming game, and Destiny, having no option but to confess, admitted to dating both boys at the same time. When they asked which one she preferred she told them both to get lost. Later however she contacted Audwin saying she preferred him. But when Audwin called Silk and learned that he had been told the same thing, the two of them ended all dealings with Destiny Hodges. Silk and Audwin were best friends ever since.

The day after the two girls fought over Audwin in the second floor hallway of North County, Audwin and Silk crossed the lift bridge to Broderick Park out on Squaw Island, where the air was suddenly cool and stank of fish and seaweed. As nighttime fell, they sat against the hood of Audwin's car, gazing across the river at the harbor lights of the Canadian shore. This crossing, once a terminus on the Underground Railroad, had welcomed multitudes of runaway slaves who came to either drown their troubles or escape them, depending on which fate awaited them in that dark water.

"I heard you been messing with that skeezer, Rhodesia," Silk said, lighting a joint behind a cupped hand. Wind blew scraps of litter past their feet.

"You dropped out of school over a year ago, Silk. How do you always know what's going on?"

"I just know," Silk said. "Please say you didn't go raw. Rhodesia Cole is the nastiest girl at North County. You know how many guys she's been with?"

"We only did it once."

"How many times you think it takes?" Silk said. He held the joint between two fingers and pointed at Audwin. "White man's got AIDS out there for brothers like you."

"I used a rubber, Silk."

"Good. Ain't no girl worth dying for. Only person worth dying for is your brother, your *black* brother. That's right. Loyalty is everything. Bros before hoes. Like how we did with Destiny Hodges. Never let a bitch come between you and your boy."

They cuffed palms and snapped their fingers.

"Don't ever waste time chasing them," Silk added. He shared the joint with Audwin, and then offered this aphorism, "Chase money, and bitches will chase *you*. That's right. Panties drop when the smell of money's in the air. Then it's all about the masses, baby boy. A numbers game. Get as many as you can. Out of every ten, one or two might be good. Then you get ten more. Don't give a shit about their feelings. It's all a game. Learn how to play it.

"Now when you fuck a girl—and this is important, Audwin—when you fuck her you gotta be rough. That's how you get her respect. Let her know you own that pussy. Put your name on it. And when you're all up inside of her, talk sexy to her. Tell her, 'Hey, baby. I know you like it. I know you want it.' When she asks you how you know what she wants, you say, 'Because this is what love is, baby. Everybody wants love.' Man, she'll be begging you to come back and smash it next time."

"That what they teach you in the Nation of Islam?" Audwin said.

"Nah. That's some original science right there." And they cuffed palms and snapped their fingers again.

They were at Silk's apartment the next time they smoked weed. Silk put on a Run-D.M.C. record and told Audwin he had something special for him. "Here, check this out," he said, holding out a stiletto switchblade. "Bet you never had one of these." He flicked out the glinting blade, displayed it, wielded it, and then locked it again and handed it to Audwin. "I got this for you," he said. "I want you to have it."

"Wow. Thanks, Silk. What made you do this for me?"

"In the Nation, we believe in protecting ourselves. The black man is always a target. More than any other person on earth. Watch the news. Most violence is perpetrated against us. Been that way for centuries. Protect yourself, brother. I'd give you a pistol, but I only have one. This'll do for now. Keep it on you everywhere you go. Never know when you'll need it."

The following spring, Silk mentioned in passing that he thought it was odd that he had never met Audwin's family. Audwin brushed it aside, calling it no big deal, especially since he himself had never met Silk's parents. "Doesn't matter," Audwin said. "I thought we didn't answer to our parents anymore."

"Right. But it's cool that your father's the mayor, ain't it?"

"No, not really."

"So what about your sister? I hear she's fine as wine. That true?"

This caught Audwin off-guard. Of course, by the term family, Silk must have meant everyone, but Audwin would have figured his fifteen-year-old sister was the least of Silk's concern, especially since she was, in fact, only fifteen. "I don't see her that way, Silk," Audwin said. "Who told you that?"

"I hear things, brother. But listen. I'm having a party this weekend. Got a bunch people coming. All night long. I want you to come." Silk explained that he was hosting a birthday party Friday night for a girl named Antonisha, who was turning eighteen and graduating this year. He thought Audwin might like her. She wasn't pretty. But pussy was pussy, and Audwin could get a piece before she left for college.

"I'll have to see," Audwin said. "My parents have been on my ass about staying out late."

"You have to come, brother. Bring your own liquor. Antonisha loves whiskey. She'll lick it right off your nuts."

"How do you know that? You've been with her?"

"Nah. I told you, I hear things."

"You heard *that*, Silk?"

"Man, don't have me throw this party and you don't show. You trying to get some booty or not? Let's do this."

"All right. If I can get out the house, I'll come." He certainly wasn't opposed to a Friday night party, and of course he had no qualms about Antonisha licking whiskey off of him. But it would come at the price of another fight with his parents, which wasn't something he looked forward to.

"Oh yeah, and bring your sister," Silk said. "I'd like to meet her." He said this with the same excitement with which he spoke of Antonisha.

This curious interest in Giselle smelled as fishy as the air at Broderick Park. What did Silk have in mind, and to whom was he trying to introduce her? He and his younger sister had differences for sure, and maybe she was a little fast for her age, but he'd be damned if one of Silk's buddies was going to get some play. "Not a chance," Audwin said. "I'll be lucky if I can get out the house myself. And there's no way I'm bringing my sister to a house party."

"She a virgin or something?"

Audwin stared.

"Don't be offended. I'm just asking." Silk shadowboxed Audwin's torso. Audwin brushed him away. "Chill out," Silk said. "Just wondered if she wanted to hang with us."

"My sister's not part of your numbers game, Silk."

"Okay, brother, don't trip. I don't even know the girl."

"Keep it that way."

On Friday, when Silk's party took place, the rain started after nightfall and never let up, and a grayish fog rose out of the darkness of Lake Erie. It had grown cold out by the water and in the city, and very windy, so that the spring warmth that had flowed in during midweek had now completely receded. Audwin arrived late to the party, though in possession of his own whiskey, which he had pilfered from his father's liquor cabinet. Though his parents had held him up, trying to stop him from leaving at that hour, he had defied them and left—much the way Silk would have told him to do—and made his way through the battering rain, and through the fog, all the way to the McCarley Gardens Apartments downtown.

Silk's apartment was loud and full. Audwin recognized players from the North County Bulldogs and some of the cheerleaders, though most of the partygoers were strangers, or people he had only seen in passing before. Everyone was drinking, or already drunk, and a dance feud was keeping up a lot of noise. Destiny Hodges swayed among the dancers, pretty as ever, breasts bouncing in her blouse as she boogied up close to Silk. When Silk saw Audwin, he two-stepped over and slapped his palm.

"Numbers game, baby," he said, winking, still grooving. "Come meet Antonisha." He was referring to the smiling, unattractive guest of honor, who was doing the Wop in front of a young man who couldn't keep his hands off her.

"Destiny's here," Audwin said. "I thought we dumped her. Are you're still messing with her?"

"Nah, it's not like that. She paged me when she heard about the party."

"And you let her come?"

"Take a chill pill, brother. I told her you'd be here. Don't give a shit, remember? Now hand Antonisha that whiskey bottle, and y'all go get busy in the back. Take Destiny too. I don't care."

"I don't want Destiny. You said you didn't either. That was our agreement."

"Will you stop whining like a bitch?" Silk shouted. People glanced over. Silk left him standing there.

While everyone partied in front of him, Audwin sat alone pouring himself a glass of whiskey, which he drank straight, and then another. Destiny's presence forced him to reevaluate his friendship with Silk. He had entered into a covenant of loyalty only to learn that Silk had been deceiving him the entire time. Audwin had given up Destiny Hodges, not because he wanted to be without her but because he wanted to please Silk. It had been the foundation of their brotherhood. Bros before hoes. No girl would come between them. But Silk had said it all just to get him out of the picture. While he, Audwin, was missing Destiny, Silk was screwing the back out of her and offering some hideous birthday girl as the happy medium. So when Silk came back trying to be civil, Audwin, already queasy from too much whiskey in too short a time, was not in the mood to talk, and wanted to leave. "I'm breaking out, Silk."

"What about Antonisha?"

"You take her."

"All right, brother," Silk said. "I can lead you to it, but I can't make you do it. But check this out. Next time, bring Giselle over."

"You're drunk, man. I already told you she's not one of your hoes."

"Don't kid yourself." Silk swilled a glass of something clear and licked his lips into a vile smirk. "'Cause Charles Vargas been tapping that ass on the regular for months now. And I heard she's a freak!"

In later years, Audwin wouldn't recall where the strength came from to knock Silk clear across the room with one blow. The drinking glass shattered on the floor as he fell. About all Audwin would remember was rushing out to his car without looking back to see whether he was being chased. He sped away into the night, into the rain, not stopping at red lights or stop signs. There were strokes of lightning now, and some echoes of thunder overhead, but he didn't slow down. The steering wheel fought against the force of the wind. His tires struggled not to lose traction. He was going too fast, and was aware of it, but a strange euphoria had come over his mind and made it right. And when he considered who might be chasing him, he kept going. When he thought about how he had lost his only true friend, he saw no reason to slow down. And when it occurred to him in a flash flood of heartbreak that his very identity lay somewhere back there, somewhere behind him, his car was more determined than ever to keep whizzing forward.

But when one has lost control of one's life, it is not hard to lose control of a car.

Six blocks northeast of Silk's place, Audwin turned down the wrong street and landed in the Fruit Belt. The turn was much too sharp, and it happened all at once. After the rain and fog ambushed him, his tires hydroplaned on the wet pavement. The steering wheel surrendered to the wind, and his car went swerving and sliding into the front porch of 99 Peach Street, the home of a woman named Loretta Ford, who for some reason seemed almost pleased to have the company.

20

Early one morning, Pritchard Jennings, an ordinary man, did a very extraordinary thing. He killed himself with his father's revolver and took Giselle with him. He had attacked her as she emerged from the Nottingham Residence that morning. Assaulted her, and left her there fallen in a bloodstained bank of snow. Eric saw it all and ran for help. But no one could save her. Her final breath had already been breathed into that bloody snow. When police went looking for Pritchard, they didn't have to search far. He had only driven to the corner before he parked and shot himself dead. Media crews crowded the grounds of the Nottingham Residence, and the Olmstead School, and the former mayor's house on Middlesex Road. Days later, under a gloomy winter sun, they camped outside the doors of Mount Sinai Baptist Church, the site of Giselle's funeral.

Cornelius never showed up. Or at least he didn't go inside when Bernadine and everyone else processioned in. During the funeral, he was nowhere to be found and was apparently last seen meandering through the surrounding streets. He didn't attend the burial and didn't come home to help Bernadine comfort Eric and greet people at the repast.

Around midnight, the house was quiet, and Eric, after a difficult time, had fallen asleep in Giselle's old bed. Bernadine retired to the master bedroom, peering out the window to see whether Cornelius was pulling up, but he wasn't. She climbed into bed and switched off the lamp. Moonlight shone through the blinds of the balcony door. Bernadine lay there staring into the dark, meditating on what she could have done to save her daughter. When it became real that her beloved Giselle could never come back, she wept.

"Did you ever cry for me, Mother?" a voice said from the shadows. Audwin was across the room sitting on the floor, a ray of moonlight across his face.

Immediately, Bernadine sat up. "Audwin, is that you?" When she switched on the lamp, she saw his gaze trained on her. "I didn't know you were here."

"You think it's my fault."

"These things are in God's hands," Bernadine said. "It's not for me to place blame."

"You didn't even speak to me today, Mother. Didn't call me all week. Don't you think I'm hurting too?"

Bernadine dried her cheeks with the back of her hand. She hated to feel what she was feeling. That she had no stomach for his presence. Something about her daughter's death had overturned her heart and spilled out all the compassion she could possibly spare for someone else, even her only remaining child, her only son. "I don't know what you feel, love," she said. "You've been drinking. Go home. Get some rest. Your father won't be in the mood for this tonight. Neither am I."

"So you do blame me."

"We're responsible for our own actions," Bernadine said. "Yes, for whatever you've done to hurt this family, I hold you accountable."

"For telling the truth?"

"For everything." Bernadine rose from the bed and peered out the window again to check for Cornelius, but not a single car was motoring down the snowy, moonlit road. She turned back to

Audwin. "All these years, we suffered because of you, because of your resentment toward everyone. Because you had it in your mind we somehow loved one child more than the other. Now this. I didn't speak to you, love. That's true. I had nothing to say. I've sacrificed so much for this family, especially you. I expected loyalty. You gave us nothing but betrayal."

"Loyalty?" Audwin said, scowling. "Throwing me into the street, is that what you mean by loyalty? Turning your back on me when I'm hurting, is that loyalty, Mother? Is that what you mean? I'm confused."

"I mean how you destroyed your sister's life, how you destroyed all our lives. How you ruined your father's name—"

"Father ruined his own name—"

"You lied on him."

"What lies did I tell, Mother? Everybody knew what Father did. I didn't lie."

"Who did you tell about what happened that night?"

"Does it matter anymore?"

"It damn sure matters, love. Who did you tell?"

Audwin shrugged. "A reporter," he said. "Came and asked me what happened. Wanted to know if Father covered things up. Simple as that."

"And you said *yes*?"

"I told the truth. It was true wasn't it?"

"But he did it to protect you."

"He did it to protect himself."

"So you did do it, Audwin."

"He humiliated me. Said I was a troubled kid, that he was ashamed of me because I was stupid."

"He said what you *did* was stupid."

"I know what I heard, Mother."

"How could you betray this family?"

"This family betrayed me."

Bernadine shook her head, aware now of a sinful moment that can occur in the life of a mother who has lost, a moment when she almost wishes her other child had been spared instead. Bernadine hadn't reached that point. She never would. For though human, with a human heart, a real mother knew how to catch herself before committing that sin. "Come here, Audwin," Bernadine said.

Audwin rose from the floor and staggered over to her, tearful. "I didn't mean to, Mother," he cried. "I didn't mean to hurt anybody."

Bernadine sighed and laid a hand to the side of his face. She could smell every ounce of the liquor he had consumed. "My dear," she said, "you make it so hard for me to love my own son."

Audwin's eyes burned. He smacked her hand away. "Bitch, don't you touch me."

"How dare you disrespect me?" Bernadine said. "Let me tell you something. Thanks to you, that young boy sleeping down the hall has to spend the rest of his life without his mother. And now, so will you. From this moment forward, you're cut off. From this family, from our money, from this house. You have no place here. If someone asks about your mother, don't even mention my name. You don't belong to me. And I have nothing more to say to you." She dismissed him with a scornful flap of her hand. "Now get out."

Audwin seized her throat with both hands, like a vise, at once choking away all the breath she would need to live. Bernadine grasped his wrists, but those furious iron hands wouldn't budge. In a breathless panic, she thrashed, fought, kicked, and clawed, but Audwin gripped even tighter and thrust her up against the balcony door.

"You never loved me," he said, and pounded her up against the door again. He anchored himself against her body. "You never loved me."

Though Bernadine grew weary, she fought back, scrapping and struggling. Even when she felt like surrendering—felt like the fight in her had already died with her daughter—she still fought. For at that moment, it was not merely death that frightened her. Dying would have been a merciful conclusion. It was the realization of what her son intended to do, plunging his hand up her gown and between her thighs, trying to spread them open for penetration.

"This is love, Mother," he whispered. He slobbered her breathless mouth with a kiss. "This is love," he said again.

Then it happened.

Not rape, but the stab. If there were time for reason, she would have spared her drunken son. But the switchblade was right there inside his pocket, and she had no choice but to take it, to use it three times and free herself from the monster that endeavored to invade the very sacred place she had borne him from.

Audwin howled.

Bernadine gasped and screamed when he released her throat.

Audwin's foot kicked at the balcony door, and it slid open. A gust of January air blew in. The snowy balcony floor glowed under the quicksilver shine of a brilliant moon. Audwin, bleeding from the front of his shirt, staggered back toward the balustrade and flopped down with his back to it. Sitting in the snow with his head hung forward, he made no effort to save himself, no effort to halt the escape of blood or entreat his assailant for help.

Bernadine dropped the bloodied switchblade and suddenly felt a mother's compassion, though she didn't approach and didn't call for help. Didn't move as her firstborn proceeded toward death right before her. Audwin coughed and wheezed, still sitting upright against the balustrade, the hemorrhage yet soaking his shirt. The progression toward death was not quick, but Bernadine watched every heartbreaking moment of it. Glared at the spill of her son's life, the ceaseless flow of blood that had within it the very texture of her own, and indeed, she did nothing but watch.

When Cornelius arrived, he rushed past Bernadine out to the balcony. His loud pleas for an explanation of what happened and why Bernadine wasn't calling for help went unanswered. Bernadine watched him search for strength in their son's eyes, holding him, trying to keep him from falling away.

Audwin moaned. "I waited so long for you, Father," he said. "In that upper room. That cold, cold room." And then his life breathed out of him, and he collapsed onto the balcony floor and never moved again.

21

Lying in his cell at the Erie County Correctional Facility, Shadrack suffered the same dream again. *Snow is falling. Nighttime is all around. He is speeding along the high cliffs of Allegany. It doesn't matter that Syreeta is fighting for the wheel. Because he is in that distant place, and nothing she does will bring him back. In a moment of resignation, he kills the headlights and speeds forth into blackness. He guns the accelerator and hears Syreeta's terrible scream. He can see nothing, and then, instantly, the ground disappears. They soar on a strong wind. And as they fly forth from the cliff, into the open falling snow, he knows he has freed himself from the obsession and has spared his heart a lengthy sadness.*

On Sunday, Loretta visited him. A single officer patrolled the visiting room as inmates in orange jumpsuits filed in and greeted their visitors. Loretta was waiting at one of the tables reading scripture when Shadrack spotted her. "When are you getting me out of here?" he said.

Loretta looked up from her Bible and gestured for him to sit. "I won't be staying long," she said. "I told you the bail is too much."

"I'm dying in here, Mama. Forget about lawyers. Get me out. We can get a public defender. I've been reading some law books on my own."

"Black men always get smart in jail," she said. "No, Shadrack. These charges are serious. You need a good lawyer. I'm not bailing you out." Moreover, Loretta explained, she only came to read from Proverbs and pray, not to argue. She directed his attention to the highlighted verses of her Bible.

The other inmates were settled with their families. Some of them had young children. Everyone chatted in sprightly whispers, not in the restless tone of voice Shadrack used. He interrupted Loretta's recitation. "Go to Mr. Niederpruem," he said. "He'll lend us the money if you ask. I know he will. Can you do that?"

"You know I won't accept money from a man."

"Not even now to help me?"

"Not even now," she said. "When you hurt people, Shadrack, there's consequences. But you always learned the hard way." She read a few more verses before she decided to leave. "Here, let me pray for you before I go."

"That's not what I need right now, Mama."

"Suit yourself. If you wanna be in this prison uncovered, that's your choice." Loretta gathered her things. "I'll let you know about that lawyer."

"Seriously, Mama?" Shadrack said. "Consequences? Hurting people? Everything I know about hurting people, I learned from you a long time ago. What about the consequences for what you did to me?"

In previous times, the officer might have had to drag Loretta out of there by her feet. For she would have slapped Shadrack so hard his head would have buckled and dropped off. "I never been in nobody's prison," she said bluntly. "You here of your own doing. I raised you according to the Bible. Ain't my fault you didn't listen."

"No Bible ever told you to hurt me."

"I didn't hurt you, Shadrack. I raised you. But you choose to act like an animal instead."

"I'm not an animal—"

"You in a cage, ain't you?"

"Yeah, because of you."

"I have to go, Shadrack. Goodbye."

"So you don't take money from men," Shadrack said loudly. "Is that the real reason you won't get me out of here?" Others in the visiting room glanced over. The officer strolled by but didn't interfere.

"I already explained myself," Loretta said. And she turned to leave.

"You want to know something, Mama?" Shadrack said. "There's nothing wrong with my ears. There never was. I've always heard everything." Loretta spun around. Her expression was new. And for the first time ever, she seemed fearful of what he might say. For indeed, so many of her secrets had hidden themselves behind a veil of his perceived disability. And Shadrack knew it must have all been rushing back to her now. The affair with Uncle Cal. The tussle with Big Bruce. The death of Mattie Turnbull. All of it eternally wrapped in the shroud of Shadrack's inability to know. And at last, he felt no inhibition. "When I was a boy," he said, "you told me not to open that bedroom window, but I did. Many times. You just didn't know. And that rainy night when Audwin Brooks crashed into our house, I heard everything. Even when the mayor came later. He offered you money. First you said no and sent him away. But when he reached his car, you called out to him, and he came back. And you told him not to worry. That you wouldn't say a word. Then you took it. You took that money right out of his hand. So don't tell me you won't accept anything from a man, because you would. You just don't want to. You'd rather keep me locked up in here like you did in that bedroom all those years. Abused me. Beat me for things I didn't even do. I'm not surprised you won't help me. I'm only surprised I was stupid enough to think you would."

Loretta ambled back to the table. She calmly set down her purse, took her seat, and stared at Shadrack. "Proud of yourself?" she said. "Poor Loretta Ford accepted five hundred measly dollars from some man way back in nineteen eighty-seven, and Shadrack witnessed it all. Well, I guess that settles it. It's all my fault. I'm the criminal, not you."

"Yeah, in a way, that's kind of what you are."

"Really. Me. A criminal. Okay, so tell me, Shadrack, since you know so much, you ever asked yourself what I used that money for, like food, a roof over your head, lights and heat? Remember all that? Or how about being grateful I didn't abort your black ass or abandon you the way your father did? Ever consider that? Yeah, you're right. Maybe I was strict when you was growing up, but I had to be. The ghetto ain't never been safe for a young boy. Believe me, an overprotective mother ain't near as bad as what's out in those streets. Right now you could be laying dead under that yew tree in the backyard if it wasn't for me. My job was to protect you, and I did that. I gave you direction in life. A purpose. Granted, I might've made some mistakes back then. I don't doubt that. A young single mother. Of course. But I did the best I could with what I had, which wasn't much. Only my mind, my body, and you. That's all I had. You. Nothing more. I don't reckon I did so bad, considering we both still here, still living. You should be thanking me, you ungrateful bastard, instead of passing judgment on what I had to do to survive."

"Your beatings didn't save me from anything, Mama. All they did was made me bitter. Made me violent. And you know what, being in here with these folks, I realized something. All those people killing each other in the streets every day, somebody made them violent too. Somebody at home. That's where it starts. They grow up thinking the way to solve their problems is to hurt somebody."

"Boy, don't dare sit here and blame me for what you did. You was man enough to do wrong, so be man enough to own up to it. This was your doing. Your life. You made your own choices."

"Yeah, but that doesn't make you innocent."

"All right, so what's your point? I don't have all damn day."

Shadrack looked his mother in the eyes. "You mentioned survival," he said. "That was your reason. Fair enough. That's all we can do in life, I guess, survive. So you'll understand I have to do the same, and that what I'm about to do is for my own survival."

"I reckon you mean once you get out of prison."

"No. I mean right now." And Shadrack stood to go. He left her sitting there, shouting his name, pounding the table, demanding he come back and repent for this impudence. But he would not.

In the years that followed, when he was older and life was better, he continued to survive by having no contact with Loretta. No communication with a mother who saw no wrong in the physical and emotional violence she had inflicted on him. And in the many years that followed those years, as he grew much older and life was much better, he was even less inclined to do so. And when Loretta was finally gone, gone forever, pitifully buried in the backyard garden of 99 Peach Street, Shadrack laid no flowers at her grave, and summoned the gift he had so supremely perfected as a child, when he often disallowed himself to hear certain things, and now remained unmoved by the voice of a soul that whispered in the dark. *Forgive me for it, my son. I didn't know.*

MORE GREAT READS FROM BOOKTROPE

Scars from a Memoir **by Marni Mann** (Contemporary Fiction) Sometimes our choices leave scars. For heroin addict Nicole, staying sober will be the fight of her life. But having lost so much, can she afford to lose anything else?

Holding True **by Emily Dietrich** (Contemporary Fiction / Coming of Age) Born in the hopeful energy of the civil rights movement, Martie struggles to live out the values she inherited by founding the Copper Hill commune, with tragic results.

A Medical Affair **by Anne McCarthy Strauss** (Fiction) A woman has an affair with her doctor. Flattered, she has no idea his behavior violates medical ethics and state law. The novel is based on solid research of which most patients are unaware.

The Dead Boy's Legacy **by Cassius Shuman** (Fiction) 9-year-old Tommy McCarthy is abducted while riding his bike home from a little league game. This psychological family drama explores his family's grief while also looking at the background and motivations of his abductor.

The Stories We Don't Tell **by Melissa Thayer** (Fiction) When fate gives Nick an existence he can barely recognize, he searches for meaning in the future he wishes existed, and attempts to escape a past that cannot be told save for in the pages of a faded memory.

Vacation **by JC Miller** (Literary Fiction) Haunted by his wife's senseless murder, a reluctant traveler confronts his past in this story of love, loss and forgiveness.

Discover more books and learn about our
new approach to publishing at **booktrope.com**.

Made in the USA
Charleston, SC
19 September 2015